MUSEUM OF MYSTERIES

A Merry LITTLE MURDER

Jan Fields

Annie's®
AnniesFiction.com

Books in the Museum of Mysteries series

Mummy's the Word
Buried Secrets
Doubloon Jeopardy
Naughty or Knife
Final Resting Vase
Out of the Picture
Caught Redheaded
Do or Diamond
Rotten to the Encore
Artifact or Fiction
Quartzing Trouble
A Merry Little Murder

A Merry Little Murder
Copyright © 2023 Annie's.

All rights reserved. No part of this publication may be reproduced, stored in a retrieval system, or transmitted in any form or by any means—electronic, mechanical, photocopying, recording or otherwise—without the prior written permission of the publisher. The only exception is brief quotations in printed reviews. For information address Annie's, 306 East Parr Road, Berne, Indiana 46711-1138.

The characters and events in this book are fictional, and any resemblance to actual persons or events is coincidental.

Library of Congress Cataloging-in-Publication Data
A Merry Little Murder / by Jan Fields
p. cm.
ISBN: 978-1-64025-697-2
I. Title
2022944466

AnniesFiction.com
(800) 282-6643
Museum of Mysteries™
Series Creators: Shari Lohner and Lorie Jones
Series Editor: Marci Clark

10 11 12 13 14 | Printed in China | 9 8 7 6 5 4 3 2

1

On Saturdays, Crescent Harbor's popular Reed Museum of Art and Archaeology usually boasted a steady stream of visitors, even in what traditionally would be considered the off months. The Christmas season tended to be deadly slow for museums across the country. After all, when families planned how to immerse themselves in holiday cheer, admiring ancient art or even modern art wasn't normally on the list. Still, for every year since it had opened, the Reed Museum had one overwhelming day in December: the day of the Children's Holiday Cheer event.

During Children's Holiday Cheer, Santa visited with every child in attendance and gave out actual presents—not big presents, but something more interesting than the broken candy canes handed out by Kris Kringle in malls all over the country.

This year, the curator of the Reed Museum, Scarlett McCormick, had been struck by a particularly brilliant idea, at least in her opinion. She'd created a special exhibit on the first floor about Bethlehem at the time of the birth of Jesus. It had drawn people in all month. Between the Children's Holiday Cheer event and the busy Bethlehem exhibit, she would have had every right to relax and enjoy her success.

But relaxing wasn't really Scarlett's thing. Staying busy was more Scarlett's thing, often to the point where she unintentionally worked herself into a jittering ball of nerves. When the museum closed at the end of Children's Holiday Cheer, Scarlett was trying to catch a second wind so she could go over her plans for her third big holiday idea.

In an effort to calm and center herself, Scarlett slipped into her office and closed the door securely behind her. She resisted the temptation to lock it, as she prided herself on always being available if her staff needed her. Besides, it wasn't that there was anything wrong with what she was about to do. There were some things she simply preferred weren't seen and talked about, especially with the tendency of some of the Reed Museum staff to tease their curator mercilessly.

She pressed her back to the door and let the complete lack of Christmas decor in her office soothe her. It wasn't that Scarlett didn't enjoy Christmas decor. She loved driving around Crescent Harbor and admiring the fun or beautiful displays in some of the neighborhoods. And she was known to go window shopping solely to experience the sparkle and bling of the holiday season. She even loved the silver and white garland wrapped around every pole and stair rail in the museum. But at the moment, she needed the bustle and pressure of Christmas closed out of her office.

She moved to the largest open space in the room, choosing a position facing her desk but a few feet away from it, and took long slow breaths. Then she closed her eyes and stretched her arms high over her head. She imagined a thread running along her spine and coming out her head and pictured drawing her posture straight, lifting her to her full height. Then, when she felt every inch of her was in alignment, she slowly bent at the waist, reaching for the floor with the tips of her fingers. When she was fully bent, she imagined all her tension running out her fingers onto the floor. Her thick red hair hung around her face, cocooning her from the stresses of the rest of the world.

She couldn't quite touch the plush carpet without bending her knees, but she didn't let that dissuade her. She stood again, reaching tall, then dropped again toward the floor, letting more of her tension drain out. The tips of her fingers finally brushed the rough fibers below, suggesting that her stiff muscles were loosening.

She imagined the stress pooling at her feet in a yuletide puddle of silver and gold. She'd begun to debate whether that image was peaceful or disgusting when the office door behind her opened. Scarlett's eyes popped open at the sound of the door, followed by the giggling that identified her intruder as her best friend, Allie Preston. Scarlett snapped upright again, but the damage was already done. Allie was leaning against the doorframe, laughing.

"I'm so glad I'm offering you such quality entertainment," Scarlett said drily. She pointed to the tall coffee in Allie's hand. The cup had a brightly colored pinwheel taped to the side. "Is that for me?"

Scarlett had to wait while Allie got herself under control, which took longer than Scarlett thought necessary.

"I can't imagine why it's so funny to see me stretching," she said as Allie's laughter finally began to wind down.

Allie wiped at her eyes with her free hand. "It's not that." She hiccuped. "Well, not only that. I passed two of the security guards talking about you on my way up here. They didn't think I heard them, so I had to stop and eavesdrop. One of them commented on how tall you are. The other says you merely look extra tall because you're stiff as a tree." Another giggle burst out of her. "They should have seen what I saw."

"No, they shouldn't have." Scarlett tried to sound stern, but Allie's infectious laugh was beginning to get to her and the corners of her mouth twitched. "Again, I ask, is that coffee for me?"

"It is." Allie straightened her shoulders and walked the rest of the way into the office. She tapped the pinwheel with one finger, sending it spinning, and thrust the cup toward Scarlett. "Congratulations on having an event where absolutely no one found a dead body."

Scarlett raised an eyebrow as she took the cup from her friend. "Isn't that setting the bar kind of low?" She took a long sip of the coffee and her stress seeped from her. Maybe a hot drink was what she needed more than the stretching.

Allie ran the museum's coffee shop, located downstairs in the lobby. The coffee from Burial Grounds was the best in Crescent Harbor and among the best Scarlett had ever tasted. And she had drunk coffee all over the world.

"After the last year or so," Allie said, "the bar for successful events has pretty much set itself."

Scarlett couldn't argue with that. In fact, she sometimes wondered—especially late at night when she sat on her sofa with a cat in her lap—if maybe her life was unusually full of dead bodies. As an archaeologist, she expected a certain number, of course, but those were the ancient dead. Scarlett ran into far too many recently deceased to be considered normal.

Pushing that thought aside with another sip of Allie's excellent coffee, she frowned at her friend. "By the way, why are you still at the museum after closing? I would have thought you'd be searching for the perfect wave, or at least photographing one." Allie was as good at surfing and at photography as she was at making coffee.

"I don't actually photograph that many waves," Allie said. "Waves are for riding. People and places are for photographing." Then her face lit up. "See? I can compartmentalize nearly as well as you."

Scarlett chose not to rise to the bait. "So you have nothing planned for the afternoon?"

Allie tucked a wayward strand of her light-brown hair behind one ear. "I do. I'm Christmas shopping, but I wanted to bring you a cup of coffee to fortify you for the long hours ahead."

"You sound disapproving," Scarlett said.

"I *am* disapproving. You never take time to bask in your triumphs. You always have to pile on new work. I can't believe you booked a fundraiser on the evening of Children's Holiday Cheer. You should be home changing your clothes a dozen times in preparation for a cozy evening with the dashing Luke Anderson."

"I have already chosen the dress for my evening with the dashing Luke Anderson," Scarlett said. "The evening I will have here. Tonight. At the donor party, which isn't a fundraiser. It's a thank-you for the museum's top supporters. Including you, I should add." Allie had inherited a tidy sum when the museum's benefactor, an old friend of Allie's family, had been murdered. Since money didn't mean a lot to Allie, she gave a considerable amount of it to the museum. Her bohemian lifestyle wasn't exactly costly.

"Are you coming tonight?" Scarlett asked.

Allie's grin was dazzling. "I wouldn't miss it. I'm excited to see the new secret exhibit. The Bethlehem exhibit has been so popular. I don't know how you're going to top that."

"I am especially proud of the new one," Scarlett said. "It feels personal. That's why I'm sharing it first with the people I owe the most to."

Allie crossed her arms. "At the party that is totally not a fundraiser. Does that mean you're not going to take the checks that will surely be handed to you this evening?"

Scarlett grinned sheepishly. "I wouldn't go that far. But I'm not asking for money or even hinting at it. Not tonight. This really is about thanking people and showing off the new exhibit."

"Well, I plan to have a wonderful time," Allie said. "As your best friend, maybe I could get a sneak peek at the exhibit right now?"

"Nope. You have to wait along with everyone else," Scarlett said with a smile.

Allie sighed. "Fine. At least tell me the theme. You didn't even let me photograph the pieces for the program."

Scarlett relented. "I suppose I can tell you the theme. It's going to feature women in ancient art with an eye to how that reflects the place of women in society."

"Oh, sounds interesting."

"I hope so." Scarlett had poured her heart and soul into the exhibit. "You may recognize some of the pieces. I was actually inspired by items we had in storage, but I was able to snare a few really nice things on loan. One was actually loaned to us by a donor who will be at the party tonight."

Allie arched her eyebrows. "Anyone I know?"

Scarlett chuckled. "You'll have to wait and see. I want to keep a few secrets."

Allie huffed and plopped herself on the edge of Scarlett's desk, one of her favorite places to sit despite the perfectly comfortable chairs available. "Suit yourself. Let's talk about what's really important for a fancy party. What are you going to wear? You want to be gorgeous when you're standing next to Luke. I've seen that man in a tux. You need to bring your A game."

"My dress will be fine." Scarlett leaned against the desk beside Allie and idly twirled the pinwheel on the cup. "And as for Luke, I'm grateful he's coming at all. He's been really preoccupied lately, but whenever I ask what's up, he changes the subject or brushes me off."

"Maybe it's something agency-related," Allie suggested.

"I expect it is," Scarlett said. "Dating an FBI agent means there are a lot of things he can't talk about. I respect that, but it's hard sometimes."

"That would drive me nuts," Allie said. "My next boyfriend is going to be an open book."

Scarlett laughed. "I'm not sure any of them are an open book.

You're the only person I know who has exactly zero secrets."

"I have secrets," Allie insisted. "I jealously guard the location of some of the best surfing spots."

Scarlett rolled her eyes. In truth, she was concerned about Luke's odd behavior lately, but she trusted him. If he had something he needed to talk to her about, he would. That was all she needed to know. She took a sip of the coffee and almost believed herself.

Scarlett got home later than she'd planned and ended up rushing around to get ready for the donor party, all the while berating herself for not simply bringing her dress to work and changing there. More than once, her beautiful black cat, Cleo, echoed the sentiment with loud reproving meows from her position on Scarlett's bed. Cleo was used to a period of quiet cuddling when Scarlett got home from work, but there simply wasn't time.

"I'll make it up to you when I get home," she promised the cat as she appraised her image in the full-length mirror. The dress was a deep blue that enhanced the blue of Scarlett's eyes. It was constructed from layers of fine tulle, which had nearly made her reject it in the store since she usually went for classic and simple. She'd purchased it because every step she took caused the asymmetrical hem to float. That had struck her as ethereal in the dressing room of the boutique, but she wasn't sure about it anymore. Tall and fit, Scarlett wasn't really the ethereal type.

Still, there was something about the dress. The bodice featured crisscrossed layers of the tulle, thick enough to make it completely opaque and respectable, but forming a neckline that showed off some of her slightly freckled skin. Should she put concealer on the freckles?

Normally she tried to think of her freckles as concentrated tan, since actual tans weren't an option for her fair skin.

She rotated slowly again, enjoying the slight sparkle from the cap sleeves that were a single layer of the tulle and virtually transparent except for the scatter of hand-sewn clear glass beads that caught the light with every movement. They were sparkly without crossing over into gaudy, and she did approve of the way the sleeves showed off her toned arms. She was proud of being fit, though genetics played a heavy part in that considering her schedule didn't allow her many trips to a gym.

"The dress is fine," she told herself firmly. Sure. But was it right for the evening's event? She was supposed to be the hostess, not the centerpiece.

Scarlett gathered her wild mane of hair and twisted it into a messy chignon. The style wasn't unappealing, but missed the elegant, put-together vibe she'd planned for the evening.

"Better go with something tried and true." She dropped the mass of hair and instead pulled it high on one side, holding the strands in place with one hand as she rooted through her jewelry box with the other. She pulled out an antique jeweled comb she'd inherited from her grandmother years before, tucked it into her hair, and approved of the result.

She spun toward Cleo. "What do you think?" She caught the cat's avid attention on the hem of the dress. "If you claw this dress," she warned, shaking a finger at her pet. "You'll be eating diet cat food for a month."

Cleo yawned at her, clearly unimpressed.

Scarlett glanced over her shoulder at the mirror again. She was happy with the hair, but still questioned the dress, worried that it was too much. If she hurried, she could probably change into her neat black sheath dress, one that had already done dress-up duty a time or two at museum functions. *Chances are not many of the people at this event would recognize it.*

She heard a knock at the front door. Scarlett's eyes flashed to the clock. Luke had arrived, so she had no time to change. She'd simply have to go with the dress she wore.

She snatched up her heels from the floor and ran through the house with them clutched in her hand. Despite the swish of the dress, Cleo didn't bother to chase after it, and Scarlett opened the front door with her gown intact. "Sorry, I'm running late."

Luke offered her his warmest smile, the one that lit up Scarlett's heart every time she saw it. He was even more handsome than she'd expected in his striking tux and black tie. Luke made a show of giving her a once-over before whistling low. "You are more than worth the wait. Scarlett McCormick, you take my breath away."

Scarlett's cheeks started to burn. "You clean up nicely too, Special Agent Luke Anderson."

He gestured toward the heels in her hand. "You planning to wear those, or should I sweep you up and carry you to my car?"

Scarlett laughed. "That would be no small task. I'm a few scant inches shorter than you." In truth, she was closer to five inches shorter.

Luke's expression grew mischievous. "Is that a challenge?"

Scarlett held up her hand. "No, definitely not. Let me put my shoes on, and I'll be ready to go, on my own two feet. I also need to grab my purse. Why don't you come in?"

She stepped away from the door as her phone began to ring. Scarlett considered ignoring it, but it could be the museum with some last-minute catastrophe. She hurried to the phone and scooped it up with a breathless, "Hello?"

The voice on the other end of the phone was muffled. Scarlett pressed the phone tighter to her ear to make it out.

"I'm sorry," the voice whispered. "But it's necessary."

A deep, hollow silence signaled the call had ended. She stared at the phone as the words sank in. Sorry for what? And what was necessary?

2

The Reed Museum of Art and Archaeology perched above the rugged coastline where the crashing waves were a constant rumble in the distance. Built in 1927, the Spanish Revival building had once been an impressive courthouse with its clock tower, spiral staircases, wrought iron chandeliers and elaborate ceilings. It had undergone a few changes since then, but was still the kind of building that wowed every visitor.

The grounds offered guests a lovely place to walk and enjoy the sights and sounds of the nearby ocean.

But after dark the museum took on a whole new mood. Lights glowed on the entrances and exits, and moonlight played over the pale stucco exterior. Shadows gave the building a sense of mystery and even a dash of menace. Though the foyer was still well lit, darkness pressed against the windows, making Scarlett uneasy when she passed by them.

She was glad she'd decided to have the party upstairs and use one of the special exhibit rooms for her new exhibit. On the second-floor landing, it was nearly impossible to tell it was night as no windows offered views of the blackness outside.

Normally the museum put up one Christmas tree in the area where they held the Children's Holiday Cheer celebration. That tree was for the children, so Scarlett ignored the silver-and-white color scheme of the rest of the museum's holiday decorations. The tree positively burst with color and fun.

Scarlett had added another tree to the second-floor landing for the donor party. It was an unusually thin tree, covered in the same garland as the stairs and sporting twinkling white lights. Scarlett considered it festive but classy. Simple yet elegant.

Scarlett worked hard to cling to some Christmas cheer and not let uneasy thoughts creep in as she rushed around with her last-minute checks before the rest of the guests arrived. She'd had many events at the museum since she'd taken over as curator, so she couldn't guess why they still instilled so much anxiety.

"Are you all right?" Luke asked as he appeared beside her and took her hand in his. "You're shaking. It's not that phone call, is it?"

She blinked at him in surprise. She'd actually forgotten the phone call. "I'm fine. Last-minute jitters. I'm glad you're here. Can you excuse me a second? I want to check the exhibit room."

He let go of her hand with slight reluctance. "No problem. I wanted to chat with Winnie anyway."

Scarlett gave him a quick side eye, wondering if his desire for a chat with the museum's head of security had anything to do with her phone call. She doubted the call was important. It was weird, sure, but it could have been a prank or even a wrong number. It wasn't as if the person had stayed on the line for her to ask questions.

"See you in a bit," she said. "Thanks for coming with me tonight. I know it's probably annoying to watch me run around."

"Not annoying at all. There's no place I'd rather be."

With his words and expression still warming her, she strode briskly toward the entrance to the new special exhibit. She needed to overcome her nerves and be centered and focused for the event ahead. She was there to make sure the people who'd contributed so much to the museum knew she appreciated their support more than she could say. She didn't want them to catch even a hint of distraction from her.

She unhooked the velvet rope that hung across the doors of the exhibit and slipped inside. The black walls made the room completely dark except for the various lights on the art and artifacts themselves. She approached a plinth that held a clear box covering a fragment of a terra-cotta Greek amphora from around 550 BC. Scarlett had found the piece among the museum's stored artifacts and was taken with the image in the side of the fragment. The profile of a woman with long dark hair and a red band around her head had captured Scarlett's attention immediately. With her sharp-nosed profile, the woman wouldn't be particularly pretty by modern standards, but her expression was wise and distant, as if she dreamed of things she'd never have.

"What life did you live?" Scarlett asked. "What did you see?" The shard of terra-cotta reminded Scarlett of the reasons she loved archaeology. The reality of being an archaeologist was far different from the ridiculous adventures of archaeologists in movies. Real archaeology was less about treasure hunting than it was about connecting to history. All of the artifacts were pieces of the past. People had created these things, held them, and treasured them. Hundreds or even thousands of years later, the same things still offered their beauty to people, at least the people who were able to see it.

Scarlett stepped around the plinth and walked past other displays, assessing whether the light was showing off each item effectively. It was a collection not every curator would embrace, gathering as it did from so many different times and places. A broken piece from a Mesopotamian terra-cotta relief made around 1765 BC lay close to a plump limestone carving found in Austria that had come from an even more distant past, 20,000 BC or before. All the carvings and paintings displayed in the special exhibit shared only their subject. All depicted women, often stylized but always arresting, at least to Scarlett.

She finished her circuit of the exhibit. The setup was perfect. Visitors would get clear views of the amazing art, and she hoped her guests would enjoy them as much as she did. Strolling among all the women of the ancient world had restored Scarlett's calm. She checked the time on the gold watch that encircled her wrist, pleased to use an elegant if slightly old-fashioned way to monitor the time. Somehow it felt appropriate for the setting.

Her guests were due to arrive any minute, so Scarlett left the exhibit and hooked the velvet rope in front of the double doors again. She'd remove the barrier dramatically when it was time to show off the new exhibit. Then she went downstairs to greet her guests.

The event began almost in a rush, as if most of the attendees had timed their arrival together. Soon Scarlett was mingling, often with Luke at her side, usually having joined her almost without her notice. She'd invited the most affluent donors, but she hadn't stopped there. She'd included people like her favorite docents, Hal and Greta Baron, who didn't give the largest monetary donations, but gave freely of their time and their wisdom. Scarlett doubted anyone loved the museum more than the Barons.

Scarlett paused to take a breath and was surprised when Luke handed her a cup. "You should try the punch," he said. "It's good."

"When did you get this?" she asked.

He grinned at her. "Careful—you'll make me think you don't notice my comings and goings."

"I'm sorry," she said. "I'm trying to make everyone feel welcome, but I don't mean to slight the most important person here."

"Allie?" he asked, his tone teasing.

She bumped his shoulder with her own. "You, silly. Now stop fishing for compliments. I don't think I've spoken to the Milstons yet."

Luke gestured across the room where an elegantly dressed couple were glaring fiercely at each other. "Is that them? You may want to hold off. They don't appear to be particularly approachable."

Scarlett had to agree, but maybe she could help. "I'm going to try to smooth some feathers."

"Good luck with that," Luke said. "I'll leave you to it, since it may be a lost cause. I'm going to get something to eat."

"Let me know how the food is," Scarlett said before she hurried across the room, sizing up the angry couple as she went.

Rupert and Angelique Milston were a striking couple. Though in his fifties, Rupert Milston had the same kind of startling good looks usually reserved for aging celebrities. His dark hair was silver at the temples, an almost exact match to his piercing eyes. He was a successful local businessman with a reputation for ruthlessness, though Scarlett couldn't complain about his generosity. The Milstons were the museum's biggest donors after Devon Reed, the museum's founder.

Younger than her husband by a decade, Angelique Milston normally radiated the kind of effortless grace found in models, which was not surprising as she'd once been one. But at the moment, her expression was almost sulky.

Scarlett approached her, ignoring the cool reception. "I'm so glad you both could be here tonight," she said. "You're beautiful, Angelique. I love that dress."

Angelique gazed down at her silver gown as if she'd forgotten what she was wearing. "Thank you," she said. "Your dress is nice too."

Wow, that was underwhelming. Scarlett shifted to say something welcoming to Rupert, but he simply inclined his head toward her and walked away, leaving Scarlett blinking at the rudeness.

"Don't mind Rupert," Angelique said, glaring after him. "He's got something in his eye."

Scarlett suspected by the woman's biting tone that her remark was related to whatever had the couple upset with each other. She followed Angelique's line of sight and saw Rupert join two other museum supporters, Tasha Portland and Maya Shepherd. Though he offered Maya barely more than the same brief nod he'd given Scarlett, he hugged Tasha, stepping between the two women to do it.

Maya edged away from the embracing pair and Scarlett felt for her. Maya always struck Scarlett as a quiet woman, and Scarlett hated to see her practically pushed aside by someone as rude as Rupert Milston.

As Scarlett continued to watch the three patrons, Tasha eased out of the hug and stepped away from Rupert as well, though she offered a pleasant smile all the while. Tasha smoothed the fabric of her red satin dress as if wiping away the contact. Scarlett had the feeling Tasha wasn't any happier with Rupert than Angelique had been. She was simply marginally better at hiding it.

Though Scarlett tried not to get caught up in any Crescent Harbor gossip about the rich, she did know Tasha had been through a rough year and a messy divorce. Still, Tasha's smile was as bright as ever. She hoped Rupert wasn't going to ruin Tasha's evening with any boorish behavior.

Scarlett felt immediate guilt at that thought. She was being judgmental. Scarlett found the man's behavior this evening rude, but that didn't mean everyone did.

"I need a drink," Angelique growled. "Tell me you have a bar."

Scarlett gestured toward the tables against one wall. "There's champagne at the refreshments station."

"It'll have to do." Angelique cast one more disgusted sneer toward her husband before stalking off.

As soon as the woman was out of earshot, Allie joined Scarlett and whispered, "There's all kinds of undercurrents here tonight, huh?"

Scarlett stared at her friend in surprise. "I can see Angelique and Rupert are mad at one another, but what else do you mean?"

"There's something going on between Rupert and Tasha," Allie said. "They are boiling with things unsaid. And the conversation Tasha was having with Maya vibrated with tense body language."

"I expect that's more from Maya's natural shyness than anything. Sometimes I think these events are torture for her. I doubt she would have come if she hadn't loaned us a painting."

"Aha!" Allie crowed. "Now I know who the mysterious donor is."

"And you're about to know a great deal more. It's nearly time for the unveiling. Just let me finish this punch Luke so kindly brought me."

"I can hardly wait," Allie said. "But until then, I'm going to mingle and enjoy all the crackling tension between the guests. This evening may be even more interesting than I expected."

"I don't need it to be interesting that way," Scarlett whispered.

As often happened, Scarlett did not get her wish. In fact, no sooner were the words out of her mouth than she heard a male voice bellowing Tasha's name. Everyone in the room whirled to find the source.

Myers Portland, Tasha's ex-husband, stood near the stairs. Scarlett recognized him from past functions he'd attended with Tasha, but he'd changed from the cheerful, polished man she remembered. He was dressed in jeans, a rumpled long-sleeved shirt, and a blazer. His normally perfectly styled hair was in need of a good wash.

He launched himself toward his ex-wife. Tasha squeaked and edged closer to Rupert while casting a horrified glance in Scarlett's direction.

Scarlett was already hurrying to intercept Myers with Allie by her side. She had no doubt that Luke would be there soon as well. Myers did not have an invitation to the private event, and Scarlett couldn't help but wonder how he'd gotten in.

Though Scarlett didn't know where Winnie Varma had been standing, she wasn't surprised to see Winnie reach Myers first. There was a good reason Winnie was the head of security for the Reed Museum. She had an almost uncanny sense about imminent problems and rarely took long to arrive.

"Mr. Portland, I'm going to have to ask you to calm down," Winnie was saying as Scarlett reached them. "And I need you to show me your invitation."

"He can't do that," Scarlett said. "He didn't receive one. Mr. Portland, this event is invitation only. I'll need you to leave."

Myers swiveled his head from Scarlett to Winnie several times as if unsure which he should speak to first. He apparently decided on Scarlett. "I should have gotten an invitation. My wife and I have given plenty to this museum."

"Your *ex*-wife prefers you not be here," Scarlett said calmly.

"Let me help you find your way out," Winnie said.

"Not before I speak to Tasha," Myers said, but his aggressive posture evaporated as two security guards in uniform and Luke joined them.

"Myers," Luke said, his voice hard. "You're making a spectacle of yourself. You need to go home."

Myers locked eyes with Luke, but he wasn't going to win a stare down with an FBI agent. Luke had faced the worst kinds of criminals imaginable and wouldn't be intimidated by a rather inebriated party crasher.

Myers cast one last furious glare at Tasha, who had stayed well away from the group. "This isn't over," he called, then spun on his heel. "I can find my own way out. But this museum won't get another dime from me."

Scarlett left Winnie and her security guards to sort out Myers since the spectacle was over. She faced the guests, all peering in her direction with varying expressions. Scarlett beamed brightly. "Who's ready to see the Reed Museum of Art and Archaeology's newest exhibit?"

The guests were happy enough to leave the drama behind and let Scarlett herd them along toward the closest special exhibit room on the second floor.

"It's because of your generosity that the Reed Museum is able to put together exhibits such as the one you will be seeing tonight." Scarlett reached the velvet rope. "This will be the first peek anyone has had. The exhibit includes pieces on loan from museums around the world and a special item on loan from one of the Reed Museum's most generous supporters, Maya Shepherd. We are so grateful for it." Scarlett waved a hand at Maya, who blushed and nodded in acknowledgment.

Scarlett unhooked the velvet rope with her most theatrical flourish. In her head, a musical fanfare played as she opened the double doors and spread her arms to the group in an expansive invitation. She backed into the exhibit, knowing the location of each item so well that she didn't worry at all about running into anything. The guests followed, peering around curiously as they found spots to stand and listen. The door closed behind Allie, the last of the guests, and Scarlett took a deep breath to begin what she considered her most important words of the night.

"Welcome to *The Forgotten Women*. This exhibit explores the varied and fascinating ways women have been portrayed in ancient art. We don't know any of the women who are portrayed in these pieces. There are no famous queens or empresses. Their identities have been lost in the hundreds or thousands of years since the pieces were created. And yet, the women continue to peer out at us from the past. As with the women who inspired them, these art pieces have sometimes been admired and treasured, and sometimes broken and worn, but still both the art and the memory of the women endure."

As she finished the last line of the speech she'd been working on for weeks, Luke slipped next to her, adding his support to her effort to convey how much the exhibit meant to her. A wave of gentle applause from those gathered in the room warmed Scarlett.

Everything was absolutely perfect.

And then the lights went out.

3

The darkness inside the exhibit room was profound. The sole illumination was the weak and eerie green glow of the exit light that remained powered even in a complete blackout, and it was weaker and more yellow because it was running on battery.

The soft rustling and whispered voices around her sounded unusually loud in the darkness, and Scarlett suspected everyone else was feeling as unsettled as she, maybe more so since it was their first time in the exhibit.

"Please stay still," she called out. "The lights will be on in a moment." She hoped she was telling the truth. What could have knocked out the lights? The weather was gorgeous so it wasn't a storm.

"Angelique?" Rupert called. "Give me your hand."

"I can't find you," Angelique stated impatiently. "Why did you move?"

"I didn't," he snapped. "I'm right here."

"We're all perfectly safe," Scarlett said aloud, hoping to put an end to the couple's fighting. She was proud of the steadiness of her voice. "Please continue to stay still until we get the lights on and you can leave safely. I'd hate for anyone to be injured trying to exit around the displays."

No one spoke either in agreement or complaint. Around the room, small lights began to appear as people pulled out their cell phones and used them to create bright spots. For some reason, the moving lights made the lack of light everywhere else more ominous. Scarlett wished she had her own cell phone so she could push aside the darkness that surrounded her, even if she couldn't push it far.

A light came on beside her, and Luke placed his hand against her back. "I'm here," he murmured.

The rush of comfort Scarlett felt from his closeness surprised her, but she straightened up and pulled on the confidence that came from not being alone. Things could be worse. At least everyone had followed Scarlett's request and hadn't moved as far as she could tell by the light cast from Luke's phone.

Scarlett heard rustling around her, then an odd huff and thump, making her worry that someone had already run into something. "Is everyone all right?" she called out. "Please don't move yet."

Rupert's deep voice rumbled through the room. "We'll wait, but hurry up."

Luke's breath tickled the side of Scarlett's face as he leaned close to speak in her ear. "Is there anything you want me to do?"

"Using the flashlight on your phone, do you think you could get to the door and open it?" Scarlett asked. "There are more emergency lights out there. Maybe with the door open and everyone using their cell phone lights, they can get out of here and gather in a safer spot."

"I can manage," he said. "But it'll leave you without a light."

Scarlett regretted that her phone was tucked into her purse in her office because she hadn't wanted anything in her hands. "I know this exhibit well," she said, putting on a brave tone. "Walking it in the dark is less of a problem for me. If there's not enough light out there, you should go to my office. I have a strong flashlight in my desk."

"I'll get it," Luke said. "Be careful."

"I was about to say the same to you," she said.

"Don't worry about me," he said with a hint of his usual teasing. "I'm the FBI." With that, the glow of his cell phone moved away through the room.

"Does everyone have a cell phone?" Scarlett called. "If there is anyone who has no light at all, please sing out."

"Greta doesn't have one," Hal Baron said. "But I can light the way for both of us."

"My hero," Greta said, a comment that would have sounded sarcastic if it hadn't been so full of warmth.

"I've got mine," Allie said. "If anyone is really close to me, we can share."

"If you have to move, do it carefully," Scarlett said. "There are several freestanding displays, and I don't want anyone hurt."

Scarlett heard a few other voices as people focused on getting out their cell phones or edging closer to someone who had one.

"I think we're all good," Maya said, surprising Scarlett by speaking up. *Maybe emergencies help Maya overcome her usual shy demeanor.* It wouldn't be the first time Scarlett had seen leaders rise from unexpected places.

"Once the door opens, begin moving toward it if you feel you can do so safely. But please be careful."

"Got it, boss," Hal sang out.

The door to the exhibit opened. To Scarlett's shock, bright light poured in. The lights had only gone out in the special exhibit room. Winnie joined Luke as he held the door open.

"I believe we can make it out okay," Rupert said wryly.

"Ouch," Angelique snapped. "You pushed me into the corner of that display."

"Hush," he grumbled. "You're fine."

With a sinking heart, Scarlett stayed put as the guests made their way out of the exhibit room. *So much for my party.* She was pleased to see no one rushed or pushed, though she heard more grumbling from the Milstons. The light from the hallway was bright, but didn't light up everything in the dark exhibit, so their cautious exit was wise. After having been caught in the dark, the natural human instinct would have been to hurry out, which could have led to real injury, so Scarlett was grateful they all kept their heads.

Scarlett fell into line, following her guests out of the special exhibit room. She repressed the urge to whimper in relief as she left the darkness behind her.

Winnie, her face showing a mix of confusion and concern, met Scarlett outside the door. "What happened?"

"The lights went out as I finished my speech," Scarlett said, trying for a light tone. "It was entirely too dramatic."

Winnie frowned. "Are you sure someone didn't switch them off? It would be a strange prank for this group, but we should check."

"The light switch isn't easy to access in there," Scarlett said as she walked back into the dark exhibit room with Winnie behind her. Once inside the door, she pulled open the black panel that hid the switches. The panel blended perfectly with the wall and was intended to avoid the situation Winnie suspected.

Scarlett flipped the switches several times, but the light in the room did not come on. "So much for the prank idea."

"I'll have someone from the office downstairs check the electrical panel." Winnie stepped out of the room and pulled out her phone. "And I want to know why no one noticed that exhibit going dark on the security video."

"I wouldn't mind knowing that myself." Scarlett left Winnie to the task, trusting that she'd track down what had happened. Instead, she made her way to the refreshment table, then faced the milling guests. "I'm sorry for the unfortunate surprise. Someone is checking out the lights, and I'm sure you'll have a chance to revisit the room if you want once the lights are on."

"No thank you," Angelique said. "That scared me half to death."

"Don't be so dramatic," her husband scolded.

"I'll go in when the lights are on," Maya said. "The brief glance left me even more eager to view the exhibit."

Scarlett felt a rush of gratitude for Maya's words. "In the meanwhile, please, enjoy the appetizers and beverages. I've heard the champagne is quite good."

"Sounds good to me," Allie chirped. "I'm always ready for food."

Allie's cheerful words encouraged the group and nearly everyone descended on the refreshments table.

Greta Baron broke away from the group, leaving her husband loading a plate. She headed straight for Scarlett, clearly concerned. "I don't mean to add to your worries, but Tasha Portland seems to be gone. Didn't she come into the exhibit room with us?"

Scarlett surveyed the landing, taking a quick tally of the guests. Sure enough, Tasha was not among them. Scarlett frowned, straining to remember whether Tasha had entered the exhibit with everyone else. She had been focused on the speech she was about to give and truly didn't remember. "I don't know."

"I have to admit I wasn't paying attention to who came in with us because I was too excited to see all your hard work," Greta said. "And then your speech was wonderful. I didn't notice her whereabouts at all. Maybe she went outside to talk to Myers instead?"

"Maybe," Scarlett said, her tone dubious. She wondered if she should ask Rupert. With the attention he'd given Tasha earlier, he'd probably noticed whether she had entered the exhibit with them. On the other hand, asking him could worsen whatever was going on between Rupert and Angelique. No one wanted that.

Scarlett suddenly remembered the quiet gasp and thump she'd heard in the exhibit room. What if Tasha had tried to reach someone with a light and knocked herself unconscious on one of the exhibits? That was profoundly unlikely. *Surely that would have made a lot more noise.* Still, Scarlett knew she had to check.

"Thanks, Greta," Scarlett said. "I'll find her."

"Good." Greta beamed at her. "Let me know if you need any help."

"I'll be fine. You should enjoy the refreshments with Hal."

Greta laughed. "I should make sure Hal doesn't enjoy them too much. The heartburn he gives himself will keep him up half the night."

Scarlett chuckled, then excused herself to head into the dark exhibit. She propped open the doors using the freestanding poles that had held the velvet rope. She'd need the light if she was going to find anything in there.

The more she thought about it, the less sure she was that Tasha had entered the exhibit, but she had to check. If someone had been injured by the incident, she'd never forgive herself. "That's what I get for trying to be dramatic," she muttered under her breath as she sidestepped a plinth in the dark room.

"Tasha?" she called. "Are you in here?" She had reached the center of the room, not far from where she'd stood with Luke. She could barely hear the murmur of voices coming from the landing. Inside the special exhibit room, the silence in the room was unbroken, as if a muffling blanket coated the very air. If Tasha were injured, she wasn't making any noise at all.

Tasha probably didn't come in here. Scarlett again wondered if the woman had gone to speak to her ex-husband. The scene with Myers must have been embarrassing. Perhaps Tasha wanted to give him a piece of her mind while everyone else was occupied by the exhibit. Scarlett would ask Winnie if she'd seen Tasha after the lights went out.

She had decided to return to her guests when the lights in the exhibit room came on. Winnie's people must have solved the problem. Scarlett was glad. At least Maya would get to see the painting she'd loaned the exhibit hung amongst all the amazing pieces. And Scarlett was certain she could count on Allie and the Barons to check out the exhibit as well.

Scarlett remembered again the soft noises she'd heard and decided to examine all the exhibits to make sure nothing had been damaged. Not that she'd blame any of the guests if anyone had run into anything. It wasn't their fault the lights had gone out.

She circled one of the thicker plinths which held a sixth-century Mesoamerican ceramic figure from the Remojadas culture. The figure depicted a woman with a slightly open mouth, which gave her an expression that was a mix of hunger and shock. The figure wasn't enclosed in glass since the plinth was secure and the display itself had a pressure sensor and an alarm. Scarlett believed that a display invited special examination when nothing stood between it and the guests, so she always tried to have a few pieces that invited close examination as long as she could ensure their safety.

She started around the plinth and stumbled over a heap on the floor. *Has something been knocked off a display?* But she knew the answer to that even as the question was trying to form in her mind. Her question was a defense mechanism, trying to come up with a nicer solution when she already knew what her foot had struck. The pool of red satin gave it away immediately.

Scarlett had found Tasha Portland.

She knelt to touch the cooling skin of the woman's wrist, but it merely confirmed what she already knew. Tasha was dead.

4

There were times when Scarlett suspected her life was more stressful than anything movie archaeologists ever faced. As she lingered near the chief of the Crescent Harbor police, hoping he wouldn't send her to mill around with the other potential witnesses, she almost questioned her life choices.

Even from where she stood, Scarlett could see how hard Hal and Greta were working to lighten the mood among the guests, even with all of the police officers mixed into the crowd. Between the two of them, the Barons were a potent force for cheer. As Scarlett watched, Greta coaxed a tiny smile from Maya Shepherd. The quiet woman was pale and shaky, and Scarlett wondered if she'd been close friends with Tasha. They'd been chatting together earlier, so it was possible. Scarlett supposed the extremely wealthy were a community all their own.

The sound of a throat clearing jerked Scarlett's attention to the chief of police. Chief Gabriel Rodriguez was a tall, heavyset man in his early sixties sporting a thick mop of gray hair and shrewd dark-brown eyes. He had a deep booming voice that suited the suspicious expressions he favored and must have scared criminals half to death. He'd intimidated Scarlett when she'd first interacted with him, but she had since learned that he was fair and smart.

"I don't suppose there's any chance Tasha's death was an accident," Scarlett said hopefully.

"She was stabbed," the chief said. "Unless you had a seriously dangerous exhibit in there, I don't see how it could have been accidental.

We haven't found the murder weapon, but we will. How close did you get to the body?"

Scarlett winced. She hated to think of the vibrant, beautiful woman as *the body*. "I tripped over her, but I don't think I moved her much. I checked for a pulse, but that was it. I didn't even realize she'd been stabbed." She glanced over at the unhappy guests of her holiday donor party. "How long do you think everyone will have to stay here?"

"Until they've all been spoken to," he said. "Realistically, this was a closed event with a limited number in attendance in a locked museum. Add to that the fact that the murder would have happened in the tiny window of opportunity when the lights were out, and we can be fairly certain the killer is right here, right now."

Scarlett shook her head. "But you said Tasha was stabbed." She gestured toward the guests. "I can say without a doubt that no one has changed clothes. Wouldn't the killer be bloodstained? Stabbings on television are messy."

"Television isn't real life," Luke said, heading off the chief's reply. "If the blade is thin and the killer is smart or lucky, there can be little blood."

"But in that kind of attack," Scarlett said, "shouldn't Tasha have had time to call out for help?" She thought of the odd sound she'd heard again, a gasp before a thump. If that was Tasha, then she'd been incapacitated quickly.

"We'll know more when the coroner weighs in," the chief said, cutting into their side conversation.

"What aren't you saying about this case?" she asked. "Why are so many officers here?"

"When one of Crescent Harbor's wealthiest residents dies and the killer is almost certainly another of Crescent Harbor's wealthiest residents, it's a good idea to make it clear we're putting everything we have into finding the killer." The chief's attention shifted to the guests again. "This is a nightmare."

For Tasha it was. Scarlett kept the thought to herself.

"Ms. McCormick," the chief said, his tone more formal than usual. "I will need a room where I can conduct my interviews privately. The sooner we speak to everyone, the sooner we can let them all go."

"Hopefully all but one," Scarlett said. "How about my office? It's comfortable and private. Since we're already on the second floor, it's the closest room that matches those criteria."

"That should do." The chief gestured to Luke. "Would you be willing to come in and observe? Since you were present in the room at the time of the murder, you cannot take part in any questioning, but I would value your input afterward."

"No problem," Luke said. "Anything I can do to help."

Scarlett opened her mouth, but the chief cut her off. "This is not a situation where *anyone* gets a plus one. Please wait out here and do whatever you can to keep your guests from becoming too rebellious about waiting."

Sure, that shouldn't be hard at all, Scarlett thought sarcastically. But she nodded in agreement, knowing better than to complain about the task she'd been given. Then she remembered something. "You said all your possible suspects were here. I know of one more."

"And who might that be?" The chief's gaze showed a marked jump in intensity, sending unease through Scarlett.

"Tasha's ex-husband, Myers Portland, crashed the party," she said. "Rumor has it that their divorce has not been amicable, and he was loud and demanding. But he'd gone before we went into the exhibit room—at least as far as anyone knew. I don't see how he could have remained and gotten into the exhibit, but then he shouldn't have been able to get into the museum at all. I thought you should know he'd been here."

The chief took in what Scarlett said, but he directed his response to Luke. "Did you see this man?"

"I did. He was extremely upset. It's definitely worth tracking him down and questioning him."

"Then we'll do that," the chief said. "But we'll begin with the group we have right here. Give me a moment, and we'll get started." He headed for one of the officers standing near the gathered guests.

Scarlett recognized Officer Andy Riggle as the chief approached him. Thirtysomething Officer Riggle could have fit in at one of Scarlett's family reunions with his fair complexion, red hair, and blue eyes. Scarlett wondered what it said about her life that she knew virtually every officer on the Crescent Harbor police force.

The chief leaned forward to speak to Riggle quietly. The younger officer nodded his head several times in response to the chief's words.

A wave of sadness washed over Scarlett. The evening had gone so wrong. "Poor Tasha," she murmured.

Luke squeezed her hand. "I'll keep you updated on anything we learn."

Scarlett widened her eyes at that. Luke sometimes pushed the boundaries for her, but there were often things he couldn't tell her.

He noticed her surprise. "I'm not here officially. I'm not bound by the same rules."

"Then I'll see what I can learn out here."

Luke's expression darkened. "Do not put yourself in any danger."

"As far as I can tell, I do that simply by existing."

"Well, exist safely until I'm back." He leaned close and kissed her cheek, a surprisingly public display of affection, but one she appreciated.

The chief waved Luke over, so he gave Scarlett's hand one last squeeze and strode away, leaving her feeling abandoned.

Stop being a ninny, she scolded herself. *You've got work to do.*

Deciding to put off facing the donors for the time being, Scarlett made her way toward Winnie, who was with a small group of people wearing the uniform of museum security. Winnie stood out from the group, partially because she was wearing a black dress that matched her coal-black hair perfectly, but also because she was so slender and significantly shorter than the security team around her.

Winnie's talents lay in her sharp mind and her extensive knowledge and experience with computers. She had a knack for designing and operating high-tech security systems. Winnie tended to be serious and professional, but Scarlett had come to know her well and considered Winnie a good friend.

Winnie spotted Scarlett and met her a short distance away from the rest of the security team. "What can I do for you?"

"Do you know if Tasha's ex ever actually left the museum?" Scarlett asked.

Winnie's professional expression slipped and a mixture of guilt and distress crept in. She shook her head. "I escorted him downstairs, but he insisted he needed to use the facilities so I left a man with him and came back here. Apparently he insisted he needed privacy and promised to leave as soon as he was done. My security officer reminded him that he'd be on camera as soon as he walked out of the restroom, then left him alone. He hadn't come to steal, which is our usual focus." She ran a hand over her face. "I let you down."

"Don't be ridiculous," Scarlett said. "I don't expect you to tell the future or read minds. If I'd been worried about him seeing himself out, I could have said something. I suspect there will be blame enough to go around by the time we're done tonight."

"I asked the staff who were posted downstairs." Winnie cut her gaze toward the team. "None of them saw how the man came in or exited."

"And the video feeds?"

Winnie groaned. "The man who was in the security office shouldn't have been assigned tonight at all. His wife is pregnant and he was trying to pick up an extra shift for holiday money, but she began having some contractions and he was pretty much on the phone the whole time and not paying attention to the monitors." Winnie tilted her head toward her team. "The man in question is the one over there who appears to be about to pass out. I think he's afraid he's going to be fired."

"That would be extreme," Scarlett said. "Especially with a new baby on the way."

"I won't fire him," Winnie said. "He's normally good at the job. He's just afraid for his wife. I intend to ask the chief to interview him first so he can get home to her. Besides, all the video feed is recorded, so it will simply be a matter of going through the footage." She raised her chin. "Ultimately, any blame here belongs to me."

"No one needs to assign blame." Scarlett resisted the urge to give her friend a hug, knowing Winnie wouldn't welcome it in a public setting. Still she felt bad for Winnie. She could see how terrible her friend felt about what she considered her failings during the evening. Scarlett didn't have the heart to add her own grumbles. Everything had come together for a perfect storm of awfulness. There was no reason to make it worse.

"What exits were unlocked tonight?" Scarlett asked.

"Only the front, and there were two people on that door," Winnie said. "There are fire exits, but they can't be opened from outside, and we'd have heard an alarm if they were opened from inside."

"Were there any doors that could have been unlocked from inside without an alarm?" Scarlett said.

"A staff door downstairs is that way. It isn't impossible that he could have left through that one," Winnie said. "But again, without a key, no one could get in through that door from outside. It doesn't help that the police have all my staff corralled up here."

"I imagine that's procedure," Scarlett said.

"Procedure isn't always helpful," Winnie muttered.

"Hey, can I join this chat?" Allie asked in the cheeriest tone Scarlett had heard in the last hour.

Scarlett jumped at Allie's sudden arrival, then immediately felt embarrassed that she hadn't seen Allie coming. She wasn't nearly as sharp as she thought she was. "How are the guests?" Scarlett asked her friend.

"Restless," Allie said. "Rupert and Angelique are still glaring at one another. Maya has finally dipped into the champagne. And I think Hal may be running out of charming stories. Also, I've met the caterer and her assistant. The assistant is sullen and the caterer is crabby. Overall it's going great."

"I'm so sorry I dragged everyone out this evening," Scarlett said with a moan.

"I'm not complaining," Allie said. "As I remember, I dragged you to the woods to relax and got us tangled up in a murder not too long ago. I suppose we're even." She frowned toward the officers standing near the rest of the guests. "I offered to fetch coffee for everyone from Burial Grounds, but the police won't let me out of this area. I suppose I'm a suspect too, which is always exciting."

"That's one way to put it," Scarlett said. "The chief will probably let you get coffee after you're interviewed. But why doesn't everyone drink the coffee the caterer brought? I know they have some. It was on the menu I ordered."

"Oh, they have some." Allie made a face. "It's disgusting. And that's not any kind of professional rivalry. It's honestly gross."

Scarlett was surprised. The caterer had come highly recommended.

"I can vouch for Allie's opinion," Winnie said. "I tried some while everyone was in the exhibit. It's too bitter to drink, and I've been known to drink police station coffee without shuddering."

"That's so strange," Scarlett said.

"It has some weird flavors too," Allie said. "Honestly, I think if I'd tried to drink a whole cup, it would have made me sick."

"Is the food okay?" Scarlett asked.

"It's delicious," Winnie offered. "And the punch isn't bad either. The coffee is an anomaly."

Scarlett studied the guests again. The caterer and her assistant stood separate from the rest, as if their status as the help kept them from mingling comfortably.

The caterer was a stocky woman with close-cropped salt-and-pepper hair, too short to be considered a pixie cut. She wore black slacks and a crisp white chef's jacket. Her lined face was scrunched in a scowl aimed at her young assistant. He stood bent at the waist, his hands on his knees. Scarlett wondered what made her angry with the young man. Maybe he'd made the terrible coffee? Or maybe no one was having a pleasant evening considering someone had been murdered.

One of the officers approached Rupert Milston. Rupert was visibly sweaty, despite the temperature in the museum being on the cool side. He jumped when the officer touched his arm to get his attention. The wealthy guest squinted at the officer, then inclined his head in agreement to something the police officer said. The movement was hardly more than a twitch. Rupert followed the officer in the direction of Scarlett's office.

It must be Rupert's time to answer questions, Scarlett thought. Could that be why the man was so sweaty? Was he worried about the questioning? Then with a guilty pang, she realized there could be a simpler answer. Rupert may have drunk some of the coffee and was feeling ill effects from it. After all, Allie had said she thought she'd be sick if she drank too much.

On top of everything else about the evening, had Scarlett hired a caterer who'd made her guests sick?

5

Curious about the coffee, Scarlett headed for the refreshment table. She spotted several cups of coffee, all fairly full. Scarlett had opted for real china dishes and coffee cups, and glass for the champagne flutes and punch glasses. The dishes cost extra since the caterer or her assistant would have to wash them later, but Scarlett thought it made for a more elegant reception. It also meant Scarlett could see that everyone had simply left their cups behind after tasting the bad coffee. The abundance of cups suggested no one had taken more than a sip from any of them. Surely, if the coffee tasted that bad, Rupert hadn't drunk his either. So what had him sweating?

Scarlett edged around the table to peek into the trash basket. She saw several crumpled napkins but no discarded food. The appetizers must be better than the coffee, and she knew the punch was good. That was something at least.

Still, the group of discarded cups suggested that her guests wanted coffee. Maybe she could do something to make that happen, even if she couldn't do anything to make the terrible evening go away.

She scanned the room, trying to decide which of the police officers present would be most open to what she needed to ask. She spotted Nina Garcia across the room, blocking access to the stairs below. Scarlett admired all of the Crescent Harbor officers, but Nina was probably the closest to an actual friend. They shared a mutual love of cats, for one thing.

Scarlett headed for Nina. Though her uniform was impeccably neat, as usual, Nina wore her long brown hair in a messy ponytail, the sole hint of chaos in her professional demeanor. Scarlett thought that summed up Nina quite well. She was an exceptionally good officer with an incongruously sweet temperament. She suspected that made her an asset whenever they needed someone to connect with people.

Scarlett was halfway across the open space when someone stepped purposefully in front of her. Libby Proctor, the caterer, tilted her chin up defiantly. "Ms. McCormick, when will I be allowed to clean up and leave? This is a very unpleasant experience."

"You are still well within the hours you are contracted for," Scarlett said, refusing to let the angry woman intimidate her. "And the guests will need refreshments for as long as the police keep us here. I do understand the circumstances must be trying."

Libby huffed. "That's one way to put it." She waved a hand behind her. "I'm not so much worried about me. My assistant is sick."

Sure enough, the young man in the catering uniform of white shirt and black slacks was clearly unwell. His face was nearly as pale as his shirt as he leaned against the wall. "Do you know what's wrong with him?"

"I have no idea. He's been peaked all evening and making frequent trips to the restroom, but since he kept working I figured it was none of my business," she said. "But now I'm worried he will faint or something. It's bad enough that I've catered a murder. It's not going to help my reviews if my assistant passes out cold in front of everyone."

"Your concern is touching," Scarlett said drily.

If Libby was insulted by the clear rebuke, she didn't show it. "It wouldn't be so bad if the kid could go recover in one of the restrooms, but the police said we have to stay out here in the open until we're questioned."

Scarlett suspected the woman meant she would prefer for her assistant to be out of sight, but it wasn't a bad idea. The restrooms had small chaises in them and that would give him a chance to sit or even lie down if necessary. "I'll speak with a police officer about it," Scarlett said. "I'm sure they won't want to make the young man's illness any worse. I don't think I know his name."

"Val," Libby said. "Val Antonov. He's usually a good worker."

Scarlett wasn't sure what the young man's work ethic had to do with his present state, but she let the comment go. "I'll see what I can do." She slipped around Libby and continued toward Nina, knowing the kindhearted police officer would respond quickly to the problem.

Nina's alert posture didn't change as Scarlett approached, but the corners of her mouth rose in greeting. "Scarlett."

"Sorry you had to come out this evening," Scarlett said. "I'm sure you have other things to do."

Nina's smile became sympathetic. "I was on duty anyway, and I love the museum. I'm sorry for the poor woman who died. But I doubt you came over here because you have no one else to chat with."

"I always enjoy talking to you," Scarlett said. "Everyone else gets tired of hearing about Cleo, but not you. Still, I do have a specific topic this time. The caterer's assistant is ill." She gestured toward Val. "Is there any way he could wait in a restroom? He could use a place to sit down."

"We should speak to him," Nina said.

"Is it okay for you to leave the stairs?" Scarlett asked.

"It'll be fine. There's another officer farther down." She headed for the caterer's assistant, and Scarlett joined her.

Val Antonov was still bent at the waist, his hands on his thighs and his lower back against the wall.

"Are you all right?" Scarlett asked as they reached him.

He snapped upright with an alarmed expression. "I'm fine."

"You don't look fine," Nina observed.

He swallowed hard, causing his Adam's apple to bob in his long neck. The young man was thin and much taller than his boss. "I'm all right. I get anxious," he explained. "Sometimes I have panic attacks. I've never been so close to anyone who died."

"Did you know the victim?" Nina asked.

He shook his head. "I saw her when she came over to the table once. She even talked to me. Not everyone does. I thought she was a nice lady." His expression grew miserable.

"Do you need to sit down?" Nina asked.

He shook his head. "I'm okay. Really. I'm feeling better. This panic attack was bad, but it passed. I'll be fine."

"I'll see if you can be interviewed soon so you can leave."

"Thanks," he said. "I wouldn't mind going home."

Nina exchanged glances with Scarlett, then walked toward Scarlett's office, presumably to relay the request to the chief.

"Did you see Tasha go into the exhibit room with the rest of the group?" Scarlett asked the young man.

"Tasha?" he echoed.

"The woman who died."

He shrugged. "I was trying to figure out what to do with all the coffee cups. Nobody drank their coffee, and I thought I should dump them and wash out the cups, but I'm not supposed to leave the table. I was trying to decide if it would be okay to dump the coffee from the cups into the trash can when everyone went in."

"Where was Libby?" Scarlett asked.

"She came and went a lot. She always does. Catering is hard work."

"But she didn't go into the exhibit room?"

He shook his head vehemently, then a spot of color bloomed in his cheeks.

"Are you sure?" Scarlett asked, wondering if the blush was a sign the young man was lying.

"I'm sure." He swallowed again, his expression growing increasingly guilty. "She didn't go into the exhibit room, but I sort of peeked in. I wasn't supposed to. Libby said it was strictly off-limits and I wasn't to serve in there at all. But I did peek."

"Why?" Scarlett asked.

He studied his feet, scuffing the toe of one shoe against the floor. "This museum is so cool, and it's a new exhibit. I thought it would be interesting."

"And was it?"

"It was awesome—well, what I could see of it was. I didn't go all the way in. I knew I'd be in trouble if anyone saw me go in there." His expression grew alarmed. "Please don't tell my boss that I broke the rules. I promise I didn't mess with anything in that room."

"I think I can keep that secret," Scarlett said. "When did you do this peeking?"

"Before the guests got here," he said. "But after you came out. I was quick and I didn't go all the way in. I promise."

"I believe that's going to be fine." Then Scarlett had another thought. "You said no one drank their coffee. Did you taste it?"

He shook his head. "That's one of Libby's rules. Absolutely no eating and drinking on the job. I can have water, but that's all, and I can't even drink that where anyone can see me. She says I'm here to serve, not to be seen. She's not going to be happy about me getting all this attention."

"Actually, she came to me to see if I could get the police to let you leave," Scarlett said. The caterer's motives hadn't sounded particularly altruistic, but if it made the young man feel better, she was willing to stretch the truth that tiny amount.

Her reward was the expression on his face, as if half his burden had been swept away. "That's great. I guess I'm not going to get fired then."

Scarlett hoped not. "Did you happen to see anything strange, other than people leaving full cups of coffee on the table?"

"I saw the dead lady's ex come in and show everyone why she probably divorced him. What a loser."

"That's all?"

He lifted his shoulder. "I saw people giving her dirty looks. I noticed because she acted nice to me, but I don't think she was liked much by some of the others."

"Who in particular did you notice?" Scarlett asked. She knew about Angelique, but hadn't seen anyone else react negatively toward Tasha.

"That tall guy and his wife both, but not at the same time," he said, obviously meaning Rupert and Angelique. "And the quiet lady." Maya Shepherd, no doubt. "Oh, and that actor's wife."

Scarlett gaped at him, then echoed his last word in a strangled whisper, "Actor?"

"Yeah, I mean, I know they're both docents here, but he also does plays at the theater. I've seen them. My sister loves going to the theater and drags me along sometimes. He was even on a television show a long, long time ago. I never saw it, but Libby mentioned it."

Not that long, Scarlett thought, though it had been about five years before she was born. Still, there was no one he could be talking about other than Hal Baron. Scarlett had seen reruns of the television show he'd starred in, *Mummy's Little Secret*.

"And you think Hal's wife didn't like Tasha." Scarlett pointed across the room where Hal and Greta were standing together. "That lady?"

"Yep," Val said. "They didn't have an argument or anything, but she came up to the refreshment table when the dead lady, Tasha, was getting snacks. And they didn't even pretend to like each other. The actor seemed okay with the dead lady though."

Scarlett stared toward Greta, flabbergasted by what she'd heard. Greta was one of the nicest people she had ever met. Could the young man have been mistaken? And if not, what could Tasha Portland have possibly done to antagonize Greta? What else had been going on tonight that Scarlett didn't know about?

6

Greta Baron looked every inch the retired history professor she was. In her early sixties, she had shoulder-length silver hair that she usually wore down to frame her delicate features and her dark-rimmed glasses. Like her husband, Greta was a popular docent because she always had an interesting fact to share about either the history of the museum or of items in the exhibits. Her normally sparkling green eyes were as tired as Scarlett felt.

"How are you doing?" Greta was always concerned for others more than herself. "This has been a tough evening for you, hasn't it?"

"Yes," Scarlett admitted. "I'm sorry to have dragged you and Hal out to this."

"Nonsense," Greta said. "We're terribly sorry about the poor woman's death, but I do believe Hal has enjoyed having a captive audience desperate for something to pass the time. He's trotting out stories I haven't heard in years."

"It would be a sad night indeed without Hal's stories." Scarlett watched Greta closely as she changed the subject. "Did you know Tasha?"

"I did, though not recently," Greta said. "I met her parents as well, Adrian and Lila Belsky. I thought they spoiled her terribly. Wealthy parents often do, I find. The parents are busy, so they end up substituting stuff and permissiveness for real time with their children."

"So Tasha was a spoiled child?"

"Technically, she wasn't a child when I met her, though sometimes she reminded me of one. She was in my introductory history class at Santa Catalina College. She was a social girl and I believe she had a top-notch mind, but she didn't apply herself. She was failing my class spectacularly."

"Oh dear," Scarlett said, mostly to keep the story going.

"That's what her parents thought. They kicked up a noisy fuss about their daughter failing a class, which upset the administration, and that trickled down to pressure on me. The Belskys were huge donors to the college."

"The college wanted you to change her grade?" Scarlett had heard such stories before, and they always made her sad. She remembered how determined she'd been to learn everything she could during college, knowing those years were short. But it had been clear from the behavior of some of her fellow students that they didn't share her drive.

"They did, but I refused," Greta said. "I did tell the Belskys that if their daughter retook the final and wrote a new term paper, I would use those grades instead of the ones she'd earned so far. They didn't appreciate it, but they hired a tutor and must have applied some sort of pressure on Tasha. She did end up passing. Barely."

"What a mess," Scarlett said.

"It was the kind of compromise that leaves no one happy," Greta admitted. "The Belskys stopped donating to the college, which was no surprise. Tasha's father struck me as a man used to getting what he wanted, who got vindictive when he didn't. The college gave me a rather severe reprimand. And the whole business left a bad taste in my mouth."

"I don't blame you."

"The most annoying thing was that the class wasn't particularly taxing, since it was merely an introduction to world history. Most of my students did well. If there were large numbers of students who struggled in the class, I would accept the blame. But Tasha could have done well. It was as if she were determined not to."

Hal walked up to them, carrying a fresh glass of punch in his hand. "What has you two so serious?"

"I was rattling on about Tasha and her history grade," Greta said. Her tone was light, but her pleasant face had an air of sadness about it. "Ancient history."

Hal harrumphed. "I remember that incident. The college behaved appallingly."

Greta patted his arm. "Hal went to the college president and threatened to quit if my department head didn't stop bringing it up. And with the popularity of Hal's theater classes, that must have scared the man. No one wanted to lose Hal."

Hal laughed. "If he was quaking in his boots, it didn't show."

Greta patted his arm fondly. "I love Santa Catalina College, but that incident changed how I felt about some of the people and the administration. I think it ultimately contributed to my decision to retire." Then Greta tilted her head. "What made you ask if I knew Tasha?"

"Someone saw you glaring at her."

"I didn't realize I was," Greta said and pressed a hand to her cheek. "I hope poor Tasha didn't see that. I was probably remembering that time and how awful it was. I don't blame Tasha for it now. She was a grown woman who'd been through her own problems. That ex of hers was a handful. I'd hate to think I made any of her last hours harder."

"I doubt she noticed," Scarlett said gently. "However, the person who saw you glare might mention it to the police, so you may need to tell this story when you're interviewed. I wouldn't worry about it too much, though. You don't exactly have a motive."

"She certainly doesn't," Hal chimed in.

"No motive," Scarlett continued, "but a story, and they will want to hear all the pieces of Tasha's life they can to understand what may have brought her to this day."

"I'll tell them everything." Greta slipped her arm through Hal's. "And you'll take care not to behave like my guard dog. You'll scare poor Gabriel."

Scarlett doubted anyone could scare Gabriel Rodriguez. Normally the chief did his own scaring, but the thought of Greta feeling sorry for the chief amused Scarlett. As she saw Greta lean into Hal's arm, she decided to leave the couple alone. She trusted Hal to help Greta far better than Scarlett could.

Scarlett scanned the room, searching for Allie, but couldn't find her. Surely Allie wasn't being interviewed so soon. She couldn't possibly be a suspect, and Scarlett assumed the police would begin with the guests so they could be processed and sent home. At least that had been her hope when she'd seen an officer lead Rupert away to be interviewed.

The longer we keep these people, the more certain that we'll never see a donation from any of them again. Scarlett winced, ashamed of such a heartless thought when a woman had died.

Though she was now certain Allie wasn't among the people in the open area, her eyes continued to track from person to person, so she noticed Maya standing near the doors to the special exhibit. The woman's attention was on the exhibit doors, and she stood with her arms wrapped around herself. Maya was such a tiny woman, almost fragile with her long, thin neck and huge dark eyes.

Scarlett joined her. "Maya?"

Maya faced her, and her expression reflected none of the strain apparent in her body language. She studied Scarlett with complete serenity. "Yes?"

"Are you okay?" Scarlett asked. "Do you need a chair? This has been a difficult evening."

"I am well, but thank you," Maya said. "Though I don't think I've ever been so close to someone when they died. I didn't know it was happening, and I think that disturbs me even more. I would have thought I'd sense such a momentous thing."

Scarlett hadn't thought of it that way, but she rather agreed with Maya. The end of a life shouldn't be so silent and unnoticed, especially for someone as full of life as Tasha had been. Even through the strain of her divorce, Tasha had never struck Scarlett as damaged or knocked down. And now she was gone. "It is awful."

"Yes." Maya's attention shifted to the doors of the exhibit. "I hate to be churlish, but I'm uncomfortable having my painting remain here, so close to a murder. That painting is priceless to me. I could not stand to lose it or have it damaged."

"I will return the painting as soon as the police release it," Scarlett said. "Though there is no reason to assume Tasha's death was part of an attempted theft."

"Equally," Maya said with no trace of malice in her voice, "there is no reason to assume it was not. I can think of no other reason anyone would kill Tasha."

"Did you know her well?" Scarlett asked, remembering that the caterer's assistant had gotten the impression Maya didn't like Tasha.

"Not terribly well," Maya said and returned to hugging herself. "We all know one another. Crescent Harbor isn't a big place, and I find wealthy people tend to be rather insular. It isn't so much that we dismiss those with less money as it is that we have so little in common."

"We're all people," Scarlett said.

"And can you say you are friends with all the people who come into your life?"

"You have a point," Scarlett admitted. "So you and Tasha weren't friends?"

Maya pondered that. "I admired her, and I don't believe I was ever unkind to her, which is similar, I suppose. She was dealt quite a blow when the man she intended to spend her life with proved to be less than she would have hoped. The divorce was messy, but Tasha wasn't. That's rather commendable. I've known plenty of women who handled less difficult situations far worse."

Scarlett agreed, having thought something similar. "I can't say for sure when your painting will be available to take home. The special exhibit room is a crime scene, and that means I will not be allowed to remove anything from it—or even enter it—until the police release the scene."

Maya's lips pressed together for an instant, but all she said was, "I understand completely. When it can be removed, please let me know immediately, and I'll send my people to collect it."

"I will." Scarlett would have happily crated up the painting and taken it to Maya's home herself, but she knew Maya would refuse the offer. The loan of the beautiful painting had been conditional upon Maya's people being the only ones who ever touched it. The stipulation had been annoying but not shocking. Scarlett was fairly used to eccentric behavior in art collectors.

She hoped all the museums that had loaned pieces for the exhibit didn't respond as Maya had. If so, it would be the shortest run of any exhibit Scarlett had ever put together, including a rather disastrous exhibit she'd curated once at the museum where she'd worked in New York. At the time, she'd thought an exhibit on how insects were used in ancient art would be popular, but not everyone was as taken with dung beetles as she would have liked.

Scarlett, thinking that everyone had their own way of dealing with crisis, excused herself and left Maya to stare at the exhibit doors. As she crossed the room, wishing Luke was beside her, she began to ponder what she could replace Maya's painting with. She would miss the piece.

The painting had been done around 318 AD, at the time of the Eastern Jin Dynasty in China. It featured a woman with delicate features and a gentle expression who reminded Scarlett of Maya herself. The figure was frozen in the act of fleeing, but had paused to peer behind her toward a male figure who watched her stoically. While the woman's robes were flowing to show she was moving, the male's robes hung straight, underscoring his strong posture. As she'd prepared the exhibit, Scarlett had often found herself wondering about the story behind the two figures.

The piece was an unusual shape—sixteen inches tall but nearly four feet long. At some point, it must have been torn from an even longer scroll. Delicate with age, the painting was sandwiched between glass for protection and surrounded by an elaborate frame crafted from a variety of rare woods. It was obvious the frame was fairly new, but somehow its strong design complemented the art.

Because of the piece's odd dimensions, removing it from the exhibit would leave a hole that would be difficult to fill. Perhaps she could find a series of miniatures for that space. There were a few in storage that Scarlett had passed over because the women featured in them had been devoid of personality. Still, they were women, so maybe it would be the best choice.

Scarlett resisted the urge to sigh. At least the official opening of the exhibit was still nearly two weeks away and wouldn't be affected by the police investigation.

Again she felt a pang of guilt for thinking about her exhibit when a woman's life had been taken.

Missing both Luke and Allie, Scarlett decided to loiter around her office door to nab whichever one of them came out first.

She didn't make it to the office. Instead, she froze in place as the room filled with the sound of a bloodcurdling scream.

7

Scarlett's first thought was a panicky fear that something had happened to Allie and that was why she hadn't been able to find her friend. She sprinted toward the caterer's table where the screaming had come from. She could already see the source.

Angelique Milston stood next to the table with her eyes wide. Scarlett suspected she might be about to scream again.

Behind Scarlett came the thump of pounding feet, and she knew the screaming had gotten the attention of everyone in her office as well. She closed the distance to the table.

Angelique pointed toward the floor. "He's dead."

He? So not Allie. The relief that flooded through Scarlett made her feel ashamed as she stepped around the table and spotted Val on the floor. Scarlett dropped to her knees beside him and pressed her fingers against the side of his throat.

"Is he dead?" Luke's question was void of emotion.

"He's breathing," Scarlett said. "And he has a strong pulse." She gently shook the young man, then patted his cheek. "Val? Wake up, Val."

"I'll call an ambulance," Luke said, stepping away.

"What happened?" Chief Rodriguez asked.

"I came over to get some more punch," Angelique said. "I thought no one was over here, but then I saw him. After Tasha, I thought—well, I thought someone else had been murdered."

Scarlett had been rubbing Val's hands during Angelique's recitation, though she was watching the distraught woman while she did it. A sharp intake of breath from Val jerked her attention to him.

"Val?" she said.

His eyes were wide with alarm. "What happened?"

"That's what we were all wondering," Scarlett said. "Are you all right? Can you sit up?"

"I think so," he said. And with Scarlett's help, he did, though she also helped him scoot to put his back to the wall. "I started to have another panic attack and I remember coming over here. I was hyperventilating. I guess I passed out. I'm so sorry."

"I don't think you have to be sorry over being ill," Scarlett said. "Do you need a drink of water?"

"Yes please," he said. His color was improving, possibly hurried along by embarrassment.

"Who is this?" Chief Rodriguez asked.

"This is Val Antonov," Scarlett said. "He works with the caterer, and he hasn't been feeling well for a while."

Val raised his eyes toward the chief and alarm crept over his face again. "I have panic attacks. It's not guilt or anything. And I'm okay. I think I fainted, but that's happened before. I'm fine."

The chief offered the young man a smile, a rare expression when he was at work. "Why don't you come and have your interview now? I don't expect it'll take long, and then I can get you home."

"Yes, sir." Val shifted to scramble up.

Scarlett took one of Val's arms.

Luke stepped forward to get the other one and help the young man to his feet. "An ambulance is on its way."

"No, that's not necessary," Val said. "Honestly, I'm okay."

"We'll let someone check you over," the chief said. "I'm sure they'll agree with you, and you'll be home before you know it."

"I don't want to go to the hospital," Val insisted.

"If the EMTs okay you, you won't have to," the chief said. "Now, let's get you into a comfortable chair."

Scarlett was impressed by how soothing and patient he was with the young man.

Val didn't argue any further. "Okay. Thank you, sir."

Rupert joined them, which made Scarlett wonder why he hadn't rushed over when his wife was screaming.

"Rupert," Angelique said. "They're going to question this young man right now. Shouldn't I get priority over the help?"

"I should think so," Rupert snapped. "Chief Rodriguez, this is simply unacceptable. My wife and I have been waiting here far too long. I've already answered your questions, and you said you would get to her soon so we could go home."

"I said that, and I meant it," the chief said. "But this young man is ill. You and your wife, on the other hand, are quite healthy."

"My wife has had far too many shocks for one evening."

"Then perhaps you should find her a place to sit down," the chief said. "There are benches over there, I believe."

"I will be speaking to the mayor about this."

"That is entirely your choice," the chief replied with an unruffled tone. "Now, Mr. Antonov, if you could come with me, we'll see if we can get you on your way."

Angelique and Rupert stomped off, grumbling loudly the whole time, though some of Angelique's comments were about Rupert leaving her alone.

"Speaking of alone," Scarlett said as she walked alongside the chief, Luke, and Val, "where was the caterer when you were sick?"

"She was in the office with me," the chief said. "That's who I was interviewing. Since I didn't dismiss her, I imagine she's there now."

Scarlett gave a soft laugh. "Don't let Angelique hear you say she was once again neglected."

A little grin twitched at the chief's lip too. "I decide who to question and in what order. Not the Milstons."

"Did Libby tell you Val was sick?" Scarlett asked.

"She didn't mention it, though Nina did before I sent her downstairs with Allie for coffee," the chief said. "I heard the coffee up here was undrinkable."

"Yeah, no one drank it tonight," Val said. "Which is weird. People usually love the coffee."

"It might pay to get a sample," Luke said.

"I'll put someone on that." They reached the door of the office, and the chief spoke to Scarlett. "Would you please stay here with Val while I finish up with his boss?"

"I'd be happy to," Scarlett said.

The chief opened the door to the office and stepped in. Scarlett peeked over his shoulder, interested to see if Libby had been the least bit disturbed by the screaming. To her surprise, she noticed something strange. The office was empty.

"She doesn't appear to have waited," Luke said.

"I noticed." The chief pointed at Luke. "Grab one of the officers out there and tell him I want Libby Proctor found. I didn't release her."

"I'm on it," Luke said.

"Then I suppose you don't need to wait," the chief told Val. "Come on in."

Val swallowed hard, which must have been a nervous habit. He trudged into the office like a teenager facing the school principal.

Luke put an arm around Scarlett to shepherd her down the short corridor leading to the second-floor landing and her increasingly upset guests. A brief survey of the landing showed Scarlett that everyone was growing increasingly impatient. Angelique's screaming hadn't calmed any nerves. Libby was nowhere in sight.

"Are you okay?" Luke asked, leaning close so his voice wouldn't carry. "This must be a stressful evening for you as much as them."

"It hasn't been one of my top Christmas events." Then she remembered the previous year and sighed deeply. "Though maybe I should be getting used to murder for Christmas."

"No," Luke said. "Let's not get used to that." He scanned the room. "Now to deliver the chief's message."

"Good," Scarlett said. "I'm beginning to think Libby is quite a piece of work. I can't believe she never even mentioned the fact that Val was unwell. I hope the chief gives her a good lecture."

"I'm not sure I've ever heard Gabriel lecture," Luke said. "And I've known him for years. But he can glower with the best of them."

That made Scarlett smile, but not as much as seeing Allie striding toward the group from the direction of the stairs with Nina in tow. Both Allie and the police officer carried large beverage trays full of take-out cups. "Coffee for everyone," Allie announced. "Fresh from Burial Grounds."

"About time!" Rupert boomed as he joined the rush for the coffee.

"My tray is all decaf," Allie said. "For anyone hoping to go to sleep when they get home. Officer Garcia has the high-octane stuff."

"Here," Hal said to Nina. "Let me get that."

"I don't mind holding it," the officer said.

"You should probably hand it over," Luke told her. "I have a message from the chief."

"Oh." Nina quickly shifted the tray to Hal with a grateful smile. After her hands were free, she brushed them together as she gave her full attention to Luke. "What's the message?"

"The chief was interviewing Libby Proctor," Luke said. "He was called away when her assistant passed out, but he wasn't done with the interview. When he got back to the office, the caterer was gone. He wants to talk to her."

"I'll find her," Nina said. "Let me make sure she hasn't gotten downstairs. Do you mind searching for her up here? Scarlett knows the floor here, and we're spread too thin to start a search on both floors."

"I'll get Winnie's security team to help keep people corralled up here," Scarlett said. "If that's okay. It would free up more officers for the search."

"Good plan," Luke said.

"Andy can stay up here to watch the watchers," Nina said. "That should keep the chief happy. Then everyone else can search for Libby downstairs. I assume that's probably where she went in an effort to leave." She hurried away.

"If she did go downstairs," Scarlett said, "she left her stuff behind."

"She may figure it's worth it if she's got something to hide." Luke tilted his head toward the group of security guards milling around Winnie. "Let's talk to Winnie's people about watching the guests, then start our own search. Do you have some ideas of where we could check?"

"Maybe a few," Scarlett said as she followed him.

When they reached the security team, Luke quickly explained the situation.

"She didn't go down these stairs," Winnie said. "And she didn't go near the elevator. I have a man over there. It was probably stretching the rules about staying put, but I was worried."

"Maybe we should check on him," Luke said.

"No problem." Winnie pulled out her phone and made a quick call, putting it on speaker as soon as the man answered. "Hey, have you seen anyone near the elevators?"

"The caterer lady headed that way a minute ago," the man said. "She saw me and turned around immediately."

Winnie raised her eyebrows and exchanged a knowing glance with Scarlett before asking, "Did you see where she went?"

"Not really. I think she went the way she came, but she would have had a couple options after she left my sight."

"Good work," Winnie said. "Stay where you are." She addressed the next words to Luke and Scarlett. "I'll keep everyone else right here. Do you need any of my people to help you search?"

"Better not," Luke said. "We're stretching the chief's orders as it is. Scarlett and I will do the search up here. Tell me, is there any other way out of the museum from up here?"

"We're a museum," Scarlett said. "We haven't managed to put in any secret passages yet."

"I don't know," Luke said. "The museum has had plenty of mysterious secrets."

"Sometimes, it does feel that way. Right now, I'll settle for solving one small mystery—the mystery of Libby Proctor."

"In that case," Luke said, "let's go hunting."

As they stood at the edge of the large open space, Scarlett pondered where Libby might have gone. She wasn't an expert on the museum as far as Scarlett knew. When she'd hired the caterer, Libby had acted as if it would be her first time in the museum. If that were true, she ought to be fairly easy to find. At least Scarlett hoped so.

"Where do we start?" Luke asked.

Scarlett pondered his question. The second floor of the museum basically mirrored the first, though it was smaller since the first floor included some add-ons to the original building.

"We should start with the galleries," she said finally. "The Ancient Roman gallery and the Ancient Egyptian gallery are both quite large. I don't know why she'd want to go into either of them, but I have no idea what's going on in that woman's mind."

Luke spun in a slow circle. "Roman is closest. Let's start there."

Since the party was meant to focus on the new exhibit and the large open area for refreshments, the rest of the galleries on the second floor were dark. As Scarlett and Luke entered the Roman Gallery, he whistled. "I've never been in here in the dark. Spooky."

"I suppose," Scarlett replied, though she'd walked through the galleries in the dark many times. She found them peaceful rather than spooky, but she could see his point. If one wasn't sure where to go, the room would be disturbing, but it offered plenty of places for someone to hide.

In the long, narrow gallery, most of the exhibits lined the walls, but between stretches of glass cases, freestanding figures wore facsimiles of ancient Roman clothing, both military garb and everyday dress. They gave visitors a glimpse into the lives of the people of that time, since people could get quite close to the figures and get a true sense of the textiles, leather, and metal trims on the clothing. In the pale light from the exit signs, the figures were less distinct, and Scarlett could see how the soldiers could appear ominous, frozen in the shadows with their weapons.

Luke took Scarlett's hand as they navigated the darkness in the gallery. "I'll have to trust your knowledge of these galleries," he said. "I feel as if I'm about to plow into something priceless with every step."

"I'll keep you away from the big-ticket items," she said, though all the galleries were designed to avoid accidental mishaps. They had to withstand that kind of contact. The few exhibits in the middle of the room were completely enclosed and even had soft corners. Still, she wasn't about to object to holding Luke's hand.

The profound quiet in the galleries convinced Scarlett that no one was in them even before they wove their way through, but she supposed it was good to know for sure.

As they crossed to the Egyptian gallery, Scarlett was surprised when Luke said, "I don't suppose you'd consider changing your mind and coming home with me for Christmas dinner with my parents."

"Has something changed?" Scarlett asked, bewildered by his asking a question she'd already answered. "You didn't promise I'd come before you asked me, did you?"

Luke laughed. "No, of course not. But Christmas won't be as fun without you there."

"We can exchange gifts the day before," Scarlett said. "I'll even make a nice dinner. It'll be special."

"Right." The disappointment in his tone couldn't have been any clearer.

"It's not that I don't enjoy your family," Scarlett said. "They're lovely. But Christmas is a special time for family getting together, and I'd feel awkward. Besides, I was planning a full day of pampering myself for Christmas. I've already bought the bath bombs and novels."

"You know my mom would welcome you," Luke said.

"She would," Scarlett said. "Which is kind and even wonderful to be sure, but I think there's something sacred about family Christmas." She didn't quite know how to explain that spending Christmas with someone's family felt like the kind of step taken with a fiancé, not a boyfriend, even when the boyfriend was as wonderful as Luke.

Luke dropped the topic, but Scarlett wasn't sure how well he'd taken her answer. She thought she'd probably hurt his feelings and didn't know what to do about it. Some things were hard to express.

They exited the Egyptian exhibit and faced a hall. "There are restrooms down there," she said, pointing. "They aren't used as much as the main ones on this floor. I don't know why the caterer would come down here when there are closer, larger facilities."

"If we find her, we'll ask her."

They reached the end of the short hall quickly, and Luke ducked into the men's room while Scarlett pushed open the other door and walked into the well-lit ladies' room. The brightness in the room surprised Scarlett. In a moment, she saw why the light was already on.

Libby Proctor sat on the countertop between the restroom's two sinks. The woman's shoulders were hunched, and she stared at the floor. She didn't look up, though she must have been aware of Scarlett's entrance.

"The police are searching for you," Scarlett said.

"I already talked to them," Libby muttered without raising her head.

"Apparently the chief wasn't done. Besides, he didn't want anyone wandering the halls here."

She raised her eyes. They were swollen and red-rimmed. The woman had been crying. "And yet," Libby said, "here you are."

"I was hunting for you."

"Congratulations. You found me."

"Why are you here?"

Libby sat up straight, stretching slowly with a groan. "This evening has been a nightmare."

"I'll give you that," Scarlett said. "Though I'm not sure you could argue that you've suffered any more than anyone else. Your assistant passed out, by the way. One of his panic attacks. That's what made Angelique scream and pulled the police out of the interview with you. Angelique thought he was dead."

"I saw people around my refreshment table when I came out of the office," Libby said. "I thought they were waiting to complain some more about the coffee. I didn't want to hear more of that."

"I'm sure Val would be touched by your concern."

Libby huffed. "How is he?"

"He sounded okay once he came around. The police are speaking to him so they can let him go home."

"That would be hard," Libby said. "I'm his ride."

Scarlett knew the police would simply send an officer to drive Val home, but she didn't mention that. "Maybe it's best you're available when the chief is done with Val. The chief can ask you whatever else he had in mind, and the two of you can leave."

"I suppose."

"Why did you come here? There was a closer restroom."

"I didn't want the company if anyone else snuck off," Libby said. "I needed a minute to myself. I've never been questioned by the police before. It was intense."

Scarlett wasn't at all sure she believed much of anything this woman said. Libby rolled her shoulders before hopping off the counter and Scarlett noticed the cuff of one sleeve of her chef's jacket was wet. The wet spot was round as if Libby had been trying to blot it clean. That alone wasn't particularly shocking. She imagined it was a constant challenge to keep a white jacket clean when working in a food service job.

But the center of the splotch was distinctly pink.

"What?" Libby snapped, having noticed Scarlett's attention.

"Your sleeve is wet," Scarlett said. "I thought maybe one of the sinks was leaking."

Libby shook her head. "Coffee stain."

A pink coffee stain? Scarlett didn't bother arguing.

A knock sounded on the restroom door. It cracked open and Luke called in, "Scarlett?"

"I found Libby," Scarlett said. "We're ready to rejoin the group."

She stepped aside to let Libby precede her. As she did, her gaze dropped to the snow-white sneakers the woman wore. On the laces of one of the sneakers was a distinct drop of red. That wasn't coffee either, and Scarlett suspected she knew what it was. *Blood.*

8

Scarlett caught Luke's arm and he gave her a questioning glance. She pointed toward Libby's shoe and mouthed, "Blood."

Luke caught up with the caterer. "Can you tell me how you got blood on your shoe?"

Libby froze. The breezy tone in her reply was unconvincing. "I let Val cut some of the appetizers. I don't normally let anyone touch my knives, but time was tight. Instead of putting the knife back where he got it, he left it on the rolling rack. I didn't know it was there. I grabbed a tray and pulled it toward me, and the knife caught me in the arm."

"Are you all right?" Luke asked.

She scoffed. "I'll live."

"That was blood on your jacket sleeve too, wasn't it?" Scarlett asked. "Why did you tell me it was coffee?"

"So I wouldn't have to have this conversation," Libby said.

"The truth is usually a lot less suspicious," Scarlett replied.

Libby snorted, but didn't speak. Luke dropped the subject. Scarlett suspected he'd be passing it on to the chief immediately. A wave of weariness suddenly swept over Scarlett. She checked her watch. It wasn't that late—the party would probably still be winding down if everything had worked out—but she felt as if she'd been at the museum for twice as long as she actually had. She knew it was the strain, and she suspected the evening would be taking a toll on everyone. She'd be glad when they were all allowed to go home.

As they walked down the hall toward the Egyptian exhibit, Scarlett asked, "How did you know there was a second restroom?"

"I didn't," she said. "I was wandering, and it was a lucky find."

Scarlett wondered if it was her own weariness, or if everything the caterer said sounded like lies to Luke as well. When they stepped into the Egyptian exhibit, Libby stopped in front of a death mask in a glass case. Since they were so close to the exit sign, the mask was discernable for what it was, though the emergency light cast it in a green glow.

"How can you work in here?" Libby asked. "Everything in this place is either creepy or depressing."

Caught off guard by the odd assessment, Scarlett echoed, "Depressing?"

"All this death. Death masks. Coffins. Dead people wrapped in rags. Who would want to be around that?"

"I do," Scarlett said. "To me it's not depressing. It reminds me that we're all linked and all part of this long chain of history."

"I suppose," Libby said dismissively.

Luke encouraged them on with a wave of his hand. "Hopefully, we'll reach the others before the chief sends more people to search for us."

They reached the large second-floor landing and paused. Scarlett was glad to see that nothing catastrophic had happened while they were gone. In fact, someone had pulled some chairs out of the storeroom, and, since they were markedly more comfortable than the few benches, most people were now sitting. Their expressions weren't any happier, but the chairs sounded wonderful to Scarlett. She could do with a chance to sit down.

"We can wait outside the office." Luke herded Scarlett and Libby along.

Scarlett cast one last longing look at the seated group, then gave in and headed for her office.

They'd barely entered the narrow hall when the door to Scarlett's office opened and Val walked out. He was obviously exhausted, but Scarlett saw he'd gotten some color in his face. The chief followed the young man into the hall, then pointed at Libby. "I never told you we were finished."

"I'd told you everything I know," she said. "I figured we were done." She tilted her head toward Val. "I need to get him home before he falls down. I can come tomorrow and pick up my stuff, if that's okay with you." Her defiant gaze shifted to Scarlett.

Scarlett didn't want to spar with the woman anymore. "It would have to be in the afternoon."

"Fine with me," Libby said. "I'm planning to sleep until noon after this fiasco. How about three o'clock?"

"I'll be there," Scarlett agreed.

"If you ladies have your schedule set, I have one or two more questions to ask you, Miss Proctor. Then you can leave."

"You'll want to confiscate her shoes," Luke said. "And her jacket as well. There's blood on them."

The chief's attention fell to the sneakers. "Please remove your shoes."

"Oh, come on. That's my blood. I explained it. I cut myself with one of my knives."

"And I will let you explain it to me again," the chief said. "But I will still need your shoes and jacket for testing. And we will be confiscating those knives. This is a murder investigation. Sometimes murder leads to inconveniences."

"I'll say," she grumbled as she shucked off her jacket, then kicked off her shoes. "Good thing I have a spare pair in the van."

"Good thing," the chief agreed. "Now if you'll step inside and take a seat, I'll be right with you."

As soon as she stormed past him into the office, the chief rubbed his face with his hand. "I'll finish with her and then wrap up. I should not have missed the shoes. I'm getting tired, and that's not a good mix with a murder investigation."

"Scarlett had to point them out to me," Luke said.

The chief studied Scarlett. "Can you think of anyone I should speak to tonight rather than tracking them down later? If not, I'm going to let everyone go when I'm done with the caterer. My officers will have collected their information and given them a chance to say anything they felt was of immediate interest."

Scarlett was surprised by the chief asking her opinion. Was he asking if she had any suspects? She wished she did. "No, I can't." Then she had a thought. "Maya Shepherd loaned the museum a painting for the special exhibit. In light of the murder, she's nervous about leaving it and asked when she'd be able to remove it."

"Is she thinking Tasha's murder was an attempted robbery?" the chief asked.

"Maybe," Scarlett said, "but that is probably paranoia over her painting. I warned her that the exhibit room would be closed for a while for the investigation."

"And you're right. Nothing leaves the crime scene until we've gone over every inch of the room. The woman will have to wait. I'll explain it to her."

"Thank you."

"Sure." The chief focused his attention on Luke. "You want to come in for the end of this chat?"

"I don't think so," Luke said. "I've heard enough lying from Libby Proctor."

The chief grunted, then walked into the office, closing the door behind him.

Scarlett approached Val. "You okay? It shouldn't be much longer."

"I'm fine," he said. "The questioning wasn't too bad. I even got a cup of coffee from one of the officers. She was nice."

He must have meant Nina. Scarlett was inclined to agree—Nina was nice. "Do you have anyone at home to help you?"

He laughed. "I'm twenty-one. I can take care of myself. But my sister may be home by the time I get there. She works late sometimes, but so do I."

Scarlett was glad to hear that he wouldn't be alone. As close family, his sister would know how to take care of Val if he had another attack. "Until then, there are chairs out on the landing now. You can sit again." *And hopefully so can I.*

When Luke, Scarlett, and Val returned to the room, she noticed several scowls cast in their direction. She didn't blame them. Technically it was her party, and she had meant for it to be a thank-you. Instead, it had become a murder investigation. Everyone must be feeling extremely put-upon.

Val dropped into a chair near the end of the hall, but Luke continued toward the clustered chairs where the guests sat.

Disappointed that he didn't intend to sit down, Scarlett trailed him.

"The chief will be wrapping up soon," Luke told the assembled group. "Does anyone here have anything they need to say before we go home? Did you see or hear anything odd this evening?"

"You mean the way Tasha's ex showed up without an invitation and created a scene?" Angelique asked. "Obviously he got into that room somehow and killed her. The man was unhinged."

"Did anyone see him after he was escorted off this floor?" Luke asked.

Reluctant headshakes met his question. They obviously wished they'd seen him. They wanted the easy answer. Scarlett didn't blame them. If Myers Portland hadn't killed his ex-wife, then one of the people here was almost certainly a murderer.

"You should ask whoever was in charge of security here," Rupert said sharply. "That person was asleep at the wheel and should be fired."

Annoyance flashed through Scarlett, making her want to shout at the smug man. That wouldn't improve anything at all, so she merely waited for Luke's response.

"Everyone in the building will be questioned," Luke informed them.

"As long as we don't all have to wait for that," Angelique said. "I'm exhausted. I want to go home."

"Don't whine, Angelique," Rupert chastised wearily. "It doesn't help anything."

"We're all tired," Maya said. "We should remember that before we begin to snipe at one another."

"Mind your own business," Angelique snapped.

Surprised, Scarlett wondered, *What is Angelique's problem with Maya?*

Maya was saved from responding to Angelique's rudeness when Rupert bellowed, "About time!" He was peering over her shoulder, so Scarlett spun to see the chief crossing the room.

"I am suspending questioning until Monday morning," the chief said. "Unless anyone feels they should stay and speak with me immediately."

No one replied to that. No one wanted to stay.

"The murder weapon still hasn't been found," the chief said. "And we cannot risk it leaving the building, so I will need to search each of you before you leave. If anyone has a problem with that, we will ask you to come to the station now so the search can be more formal."

Again no one wanted a trip to the station, though Angelique said, "I will not have some strange man searching my person."

"Officer Nina Garcia will conduct the searches of female guests," the chief said.

"I still hate this," Angelique wailed. "It's demeaning. I do not appreciate being treated like a criminal."

"Be quiet," Rupert said. "You will comply so we can get out of here."

"I will," Angelique said sullenly. "But I *won't* be happy about it."

"It would be rather concerning if you were," Maya said with a hint of amusement.

Scarlett hadn't thought of Maya as being prone to jokes or teasing, so the remark was a surprise. She was seeing new sides of her donors this evening.

With more grumbles, the guests were quickly escorted to the office for privacy during the searches by Officer Garcia and Officer Riggle. A small rebellion threatened when Libby and Val were searched first so the young man could go home, but a single glare from the chief quelled the group. No one wanted anything to slow the process.

The chief spoke quietly to Luke, and Scarlett drifted away. It wasn't that she wasn't interested in the investigation. Mostly she felt overwhelmed and simply didn't have room for one more layer of stress. Allie, Greta, and Hal came over to join her.

"Can we help with anything?" Allie asked.

"No thanks. You three were guests too. You go on home as soon as the chief lets you. I plan to do the same."

Both Allie and Greta gave her comforting hugs, then her friends joined the queue at the hallway to be searched and sent home. The warm feeling from the hug lasted exactly as long as it took for the chief to step over to her side.

"The special exhibit room is off-limits to everyone," he said. "Including you and other museum staff. Other than that room, you'll be free to open the rest of the museum on Monday."

"That's great," Scarlett said, surprised that she hadn't even wondered about that.

Luke joined them, putting an arm around her.

Do I really look so shaky?

The chief almost smiled at the sight of Luke's arm bracing her, but then he focused on Scarlett and his tone was purely professional, "Can you post one of your security people outside the room during all open hours until the scene is released? I don't want curiosity seekers to cross the tape."

"That won't be a problem. I'll tell Winnie right away."

"I've already spoken to her," the chief said. "She's been a big help."

"She's the best," Scarlett said.

The chief murmured agreement, then held out his hand to Luke. "By the way, I heard about the promotion. Congratulations."

"Thanks." Luke shook the man's hand and the chief walked away, leaving Scarlett to gape at Luke. What promotion was the chief talking about, and why hadn't Luke spoken with her about it? Then a horrifying thought struck her. FBI agents moved all over the country. Could that be why Luke hadn't brought it up? Had he not wanted to ruin her Christmas?

"What needs to be done before you can leave?" Luke asked, the question cutting through the fog in Scarlett's brain.

What she really wanted to do was demand information about the promotion, but maybe that would be better handled when they were alone, especially if it really wasn't something she'd enjoy hearing. So instead, she merely said, "I should clean up the catering table. I don't want to leave food out."

They made their way to the table, and Scarlett began stacking plates. She gave up on her plan to wait on quizzing him until they were in private. No one was particularly close to the table, after all. "Do I owe you a congratulations too?"

"What?" he asked as he held up a half-empty coffee cup and sniffed it.

"Your promotion."

"I wish he hadn't said that. I planned on talking to you about that after your event." He raised the cup. "Did you taste the coffee at all?"

Scarlett wanted to press for more information on the promotion, but she trusted Luke to share his news when the time was right. "No and with so much of it here in cups, I'm not eager to either." She shook her head. "I made a poor choice of caterers, and not simply because the coffee was bad."

"I suspect Libby Proctor is an accomplished liar," Luke said. "I need to take a sample of this coffee. Do you have any kind of sterile container?"

"Actually I do," Scarlett said. "Sometimes we have to do extensive testing downstairs so I have a huge store of them, including a few in my office."

"In that case, I will need enough for samples. Maybe one from one of these cups and another from the coffee urn itself." He set a cup aside.

"Why are you interested in the coffee?" she asked. "Tasha was stabbed, not poisoned."

"It could have been both," he said. "We have no way of knowing, but I'm mostly interested because it's an anomaly. Val said the coffee is normally quite popular, but tonight it was so bad no one finished a cup. I want to know why."

"Makes sense," Scarlett said. "I can fetch the vials from the office as soon as the police are done searching the guests." Again she felt a wave of gloom about how horribly wrong the evening had gone.

"That's my girl," he said with a grin. "Always prepared."

"Archaeologists have to be."

Before she could head for the office, Luke picked up another cup. "What do you want me to do with the coffee I don't need?"

"The punch is nearly gone," Scarlett said. "We can dump it in the punch bowl and then carry the bowl to the restroom. That'll save us half a dozen trips holding coffee cups."

"You're free to use the office now," Nina called as she and Andy emerged from the hallway. "All the guests are on their way."

"Good," Scarlett said. "I know they all have had more than enough of being here. Thanks."

Nina waved, and the two officers headed for the stairs.

"I'll grab those vials," Scarlett said.

"I'll go with you." When she raised her eyebrows at him, he added, "I'm oddly reluctant to let you out of my sight tonight. Past experience with unsolved murders has taught me to be jumpy where you're concerned."

"I'm fine," Scarlett insisted, but she really didn't mind him joining her. She loved the museum, but even she was getting sick of being there, so they walked in companionable silence down the short hall.

In the office, she pulled open her desk drawer and retrieved two glass vials. "Will these do?"

He took them both. "Perfectly."

The word was barely out of his mouth before they heard a crash from the foyer they'd just left. They rushed out to find the coffee urn on the floor. Lying on top of it were broken shards of the punch bowl adding its own contents to the pool of coffee and making a huge, dark stain on the pale marble floor.

Scarlett stared at it, frozen in shock. Someone did not want them taking samples of that coffee. But why?

9

"Scarlett, this way!" Luke shouted.

Scarlett snapped out of her daze and followed him as he ran to the stairs. She saw a flash of movement ahead of them. Someone was running down the steps. They thundered behind and soon closed the gap enough to see they were chasing Libby Proctor. As she was considerably shorter and stouter than Scarlett or Luke, they were gaining rapidly. Then Libby stumbled and fell, rolling head over heels for the last couple steps and ending in a heap at the bottom.

Scarlett was at the woman's side in seconds. "Libby, are you all right?"

Libby groaned and rolled to glare at Scarlett.

"What are you doing here?" Luke demanded.

Libby didn't answer that either.

Scarlett felt the woman's condition ought to be their first priority. "Can you stand?"

"I can stand," Libby growled. She struggled to her feet, refusing any help. Her stance as she glared defiantly at them suggested she was in some pain, but Scarlett couldn't force the woman to let her help.

"Ms. Proctor," Luke said firmly, "you have exactly one chance to explain why you came up here again, apparently for the purpose of knocking over the coffee urn. If I don't believe what I hear, you will get to answer the same question again at the police station."

Libby's gaze flicked from Luke to Scarlett to the space between them.

"I don't think you're in any condition to outrun us," Scarlett said.

"Didn't say I was going to try," Libby grumbled. "Fine, I'll tell you. But I want to sit down."

"I don't blame you," Scarlett said. "There's a bench right over there." She reached out to offer the woman her hand again but Libby limped over to the bench and sat heavily.

"Time to talk," Luke said.

"Your compassion is touching," Libby said.

"My compassion is tired," Luke replied. "And you're already getting all that I have. You can tell because I haven't called for a police officer to haul you down to the station."

Libby scowled at him, then focused pointedly on Scarlett. "When Val and I left, he was practically sweating guilt. At first I thought he felt bad about getting sick. I knew he had some emotional problems when I hired him, but he's always been a good worker. But he hasn't been acting like himself all evening."

Out of the corner of her eye, Scarlett could see Luke tensing with impatience at the woman's slow revelation. "Did you ask him about it?"

"I did," Libby said. "In fact, while I was putting on my spare pair of sneakers, I told him he wasn't getting in my van until he spilled exactly what was going on. So he did."

"And what was it?" Luke asked.

Libby directed her answer at Scarlett as if she'd been the one to ask the question. "He fell apart and started crying. He admitted to having let Myers Portland into the building. He also dumped something in the coffee though he didn't know exactly what it was. And he switched off the lights. He was paid to do it."

"By Myers?" Luke asked.

Libby finally met his eyes. "He said Myers approached him after our last job before this one. He knew about this party and that we'd been hired to work it. He wasn't invited, and he gave Val some story about how he'd donated so much money and didn't even get to come to the party because his ex was being unreasonable. He said all he really wanted was to make up with his ex-wife, and this party would be the perfect romantic setting to do it. He told Val he had a grand gesture planned. Val bought the whole thing. He's young and watches too many movies, if you ask me."

"Did Val say why he wanted the coffee ruined or the lights off?" Scarlett asked.

Libby shook her head. "Val said Myers didn't ask for that part when he gave him the money to let him in. A day or so after talking to Myers, Val got an envelope of money in his mailbox along with a note that told him where to find the switch to turn off the lights. The envelope included a tiny packet of powder that Val was supposed to put in the coffee. He figured it was still Myers, and that it was all connected somehow to the grand romantic gesture he mentioned. Val didn't expect anyone to get hurt, which is why he fell apart."

"That's ridiculous," Scarlett said. "What did he think would happen if he dumped something in the coffee urn?"

"Yeah, I asked him the same question," Libby said. "Val said he didn't think about it much. Then when no one was willing to drink the coffee, he figured maybe the grand romantic gesture was supposed to happen with Myers coming to the rescue with good coffee, but maybe getting thrown out fouled his mood and that's why he didn't go get coffee. And why he killed his ex-wife instead."

"That's quite a stretch," Scarlett said. "Especially considering the lights going out was necessary for the murder."

"I noticed that," Libby said. "And I fired Val, in case you were wondering. I also didn't give him a ride home. He's in the van right now."

"If this is all Val's doing," Luke said. "Why did you dump the coffee?"

"You've got to be kidding. That's obvious. The tainted coffee reflects poorly on me. I hired someone who poisons coffee for money. I'll never get another job in this town if that comes out. I figured if I got rid of the coffee, the cops would focus on the lights and the murder and maybe leave me out of it."

"On the off chance Val decided not to wait around in your van, I'll need his address," Luke said.

Scarlett could tell his interest in Libby was waning. Apparently, so could she, because the caterer relaxed marginally and rattled off Val's address.

"Thank you. You and I should go outside and collect Val." Luke turned to Scarlett. "Before we leave for the night, I want to take that urn with us. Any dregs in it need to be tested, but first, let's talk to Val."

They walked out to the van, where Val leaned against the side of the vehicle with his arms wrapped around himself. The evening air was chilly, and Scarlett didn't blame him for the misery written on his face.

Luke quirked a finger at Val. "You need to come with us."

Val's eyes widened and his pleading gaze flashed to Libby.

She shrugged at him. "They caught me after I dumped the coffee. I had no intention of covering for you in that situation."

Val's panicky expression landed on Luke. "I didn't know anyone was going to get hurt."

"I believe you," Scarlett said. "But we need to know exactly what happened."

Val creased his forehead. "I thought she told you."

"And now we want you to tell us too," Luke said. "Libby, you can go. But when the police ask you more questions, I suggest you don't hold anything back."

Her face showed she wasn't happy to be reminded that the police would be speaking to her again, but she didn't argue. She nudged

Val away from the side of the van and got in. Before she closed the door, she told Scarlett, "I'll still be here tomorrow afternoon to get my things."

"Good," Scarlett said. "We're not a storage company."

Libby actually laughed at that. "I thought that's exactly what a museum was." Before Scarlett could respond, Libby slammed the van door and started the van.

"We should all go inside," Scarlett said. "Val is half-frozen and you wanted to get the urn."

Val shuddered. "I was really hoping to go home."

"And if you're lucky," Luke said, "you'll get to. After we chat."

Val hung his head and trudged inside with them.

The warmth of the museum lobby wrapped around Scarlett like a hug. Her dress had been designed for beauty, not warmth, so the cold parking lot had chilled her.

As they crossed the lobby to the stairs, Luke began the questioning. "What did Myers tell you about his plan?"

"Only that he wanted to patch things up with his ex-wife," Val said. "He said he knew now that he'd taken her for granted, but he was going to make it right."

"Did he sound angry about his divorce?" Scarlett asked.

Val shook his head. "He sounded sad. I felt bad for him."

"He sounded angry when he was here," Scarlett noted.

Val nodded. "I saw that. That's when I started to get nervous. I thought he'd be different. But I'd already put the stuff in the coffee, and he didn't act all that mad at his wife. He sounded mad at everyone else. So I went ahead and did the light thing."

"What door did you let him in?" Luke asked.

"He gave me a map." Val pulled a paper out of the pocket of his jeans and handed it over. A rough map of the first floor had been drawn on it in pencil, showing the path to one of the doors that no one guarded because it was alarmed.

"What did you do about the alarm?" Scarlett asked.

"Nothing. He said if the alarm went off, I should say I needed some fresh air."

Scarlett pressed her lips together. The plan sounded awfully risky. On top of everything, she had to wonder why the alarm hadn't gone off. That suggested an inside job, which was something Scarlett hated to consider. The idea that any of the staff had taken part in a murder was absurd. They'd learned a lot since last Christmas when a newly hired security guard proved to be a thief, and she seriously doubted Winnie would let anyone capable of that kind of wrongdoing through her vetting process again.

They started up the steps to the second floor. "Was Myers waiting at the door when you opened it?" Luke asked Val.

"He was. I was going to tell him about the coffee and ask him a question about the second map he'd put in the envelope I got, the one that showed how to switch off the lights from a panel downstairs, but he shushed me and waved me off." Val shrugged. "I didn't want to get caught with him so I left."

"How did you cut the lights?" Luke asked.

"I went downstairs when you were gathering everyone up to go into the exhibit. Libby had gone to the restroom because she stuck herself with a knife." Val winced. "Actually that was my fault. It wasn't on purpose, but I was nervous about what I was going to do, and I left the knife out."

"We heard about that," Scarlett said. "You said you knew about the breaker box because of Myers's map?"

"This second one." Val pulled a crumpled paper out of the pocket of his pants and handed it to Luke. "It was in my mailbox with the second wad of money. I figured Myers was still working out his plan so that's why he had more parts. I almost didn't do the lights after he acted so obnoxious. I thought the whole thing was getting out of hand, but I'd already done the coffee, so I figured maybe I'd better. I honestly had no idea anyone would get hurt."

"Yeah," Luke said. "You told us that." They reached the top of the stairs, and Luke stopped to straighten the map. He frowned at it. "Check this out." He held it where Scarlett could see it.

She realized why he had frowned. The first map had been rough, drawn with sketchy broken lines in pencil, which had allowed the map to smudge in spots. The second map was the exact opposite. It was precise and carefully drawn in ink with clear details noted in a small, neat print so Val would know exactly where the box was. Luke flipped it over and Scarlett saw a second detailed drawing on the back, this one of the panel itself, noting exactly which switch to flip.

"That's quite a contrast," Scarlett said. "Could they even have been done by the same person?"

"I noticed they were different," Val cut in. "I thought maybe Myers was drinking when he made the first one. Especially since he smelled like beer when I opened the door for him. I figured he must have made the second one at a different time."

"Or someone could have made it for him," Luke said.

Scarlett's stomach clenched at Luke's remark, concerned that Luke might be thinking the murder was at least partly an inside job.

"Let me see the note that came with this map," Luke said.

"I don't have it," Val replied. "It's at my apartment. I didn't need the note tonight, just the map. The note wasn't exactly long."

"I'll want to see that when we take you home."

"Sure."

Luke peppered Val with a few more questions as he picked up the urn to take with him. Since they were already there, Scarlett did what she could to mop up the spilled coffee on the beautiful marble floor. She managed to clean up the puddle, but suspected it was going to take some strong cleaning products to remove the stain completely.

"You ready to go?" Luke asked.

"I sure am," Val said, then blushed when Luke raised an eyebrow at him. "You weren't talking to me."

"It's okay, Val." Scarlett dropped a wad of sodden napkins in the trash. "I think we're all eager to get home at this point."

Trying to push away a creeping depression, she followed Luke and Val out of the museum. Luke settled the coffee urn into the trunk of his Volvo, then unlocked the car and opened the passenger door for Scarlett. "You're in the back seat, Val," he said.

"Are you taking me home?" he asked.

"After I take Scarlett home," Luke said.

Scarlett loved the thought of going straight home. More than anything, she wanted to be home in bed with a warm cat purring in her ear, but she didn't want to end the evening without a private moment with Luke. "I'm good. Let's take Val first."

Luke questioned her with his eyes. "You sure?"

"No. I'm exhausted. But let's do it anyway."

Other than an occasional direction from Val, the car was quiet. Several minutes later, they arrived at their destination. Val lived in an older house that had been converted into a few small apartments.

"We'll walk you in," Luke said.

"I can manage," Val said.

"I insist. As I told you at the museum, I want to see that note."

"Right."

Scarlett wanted to see the note too, so she climbed out of the car despite her fatigue and joined the two men up the sidewalk to the house.

"My door is on the side." Val circled the house, then stopped suddenly. "Hey, I didn't leave that open."

"Hold on." Luke pushed Val gently to one side and crept up to the door.

Scarlett stood next to Val, her heart in her throat.

"FBI!" Luke barked, then slammed the door open and rushed in.

Scarlett stood on the shadowy path with her hand at her throat, waiting with tense muscles for the sound of some kind of scuffle inside, but she didn't hear anything.

Finally, Luke popped his head out. "You can come in."

Scarlett and Val closed the distance quickly. The second they came through the door, Val gave a yell. "What happened in here?"

Scarlett had the same question. The apartment was a mess. Someone had been inside and thoroughly ransacked the place.

10

"Don't touch anything until we clear this place," Luke warned.

They stepped through the door and Scarlett marveled at the mess on the floor. Papers and books were scattered all over the cozy living room. She wouldn't have pegged Val for a big reader, so the sight of all the books actually made her think better of him, even as he hid behind her.

As soon as they stepped farther into the small room, Luke touched Scarlett's arm and said, "At least stay behind me, okay?"

She nodded, and they moved silently from room to room, pushing open doors and checking inside. Whoever had been in the apartment had dragged the mattresses off the beds, torn open sofa cushions and dumped every drawer and trash can.

"Who did this?" Val said, his voice so low Scarlett could barely hear him.

She spun to face him. "You have no ideas?"

He shook his head. "I don't understand any of this."

"The chief will need to know about this," Luke said. "I'm going to call the police."

"The police?" Val asked, and Scarlett suspected he was near tears.

"This is serious, don't you think?" Luke asked. "Tell me, where did you put the note that directed you to switch off the lights and poison the coffee?"

"Poison?" Val yelped. "I didn't put poison in anything. It couldn't have been poison. Almost everyone tasted it, and no one acted sick."

"I still want to see the note."

"I put it in the kitchen drawer," Val said. "Everything goes in there. My sister calls it the junk drawer." He must have realized then that he was babbling, because he snapped his mouth shut.

"Show me," Luke said.

Val led them into the kitchen and stopped, swallowing hard again before pointing at a cabinet. "The drawer that goes there." He studied the mess on the floor. "I think it's that one."

All of the kitchen drawers were on the floor in a pile. Much of their contents were scattered around, and scraps of paper were mixed with kitchen utensils.

"Find the note," Luke said.

Val sat on the floor and began digging through the papers.

Scarlett crouched to peer into the deep recess where the drawer belonged. There wasn't much chance the note would be there, but she thought of all the times she'd put something in an overfull drawer and had it vanish, only to reappear at some point when she removed the drawer. Her optimism wasn't rewarded. As she straightened again, her knees cracked, and she couldn't help but groan.

"You can go home if you want," Luke said.

"You're my ride."

He pulled his keys from his pocket and held them out. "I'll have an officer drop me off at your place after we're done going over this mess. I can pick up my car then. Unless that will be too late."

The thought of being home was so appealing that Scarlett couldn't bring herself to refuse. "That'll be fine. See you then." She accepted the keys and pivoted to leave, patting Val on the shoulder on the way out.

Once she was behind the wheel, she realized how tired she really was. She drove home slowly, taking care at every corner. As soon as she pulled up in front of her house, she shut off the car and let exhaustion wash over her. She knew she couldn't go straight to bed, much as the idea sounded heavenly. She would simply sit and cuddle Cleo until Luke got there. "That's a plan," she said and opened the door. That's when the overhead light illuminated a paper shoved into the console.

"That paper is none of my concern," she said firmly, but she found herself unable to pull her attention from it. It was probably nothing. But it was so incongruous in Luke's neat car, and she'd had a long night and was in no condition to resist curiosity's lure. She plucked up the paper and unfolded it.

In the dim overhead light, the words were difficult to read, but she realized the letter offered the promotion the police chief had congratulated Luke about, a promotion that came with a transfer to Virginia. She gasped aloud when she saw the starting date for the new job. *January first!*

"That's why he didn't want to tell me about it," she whispered. Luke was leaving *soon*.

Tears blurred her vision as she folded the letter and stuffed it back where she'd found it. She didn't want Luke to know she had been snooping. Surely he would tell her soon.

"Why not tell me as soon as he knew?" she whispered. Then she realized the answer. He didn't want to ruin her Christmas. Luke was thoughtful that way. He probably wanted them to have one last nice holiday together. That's why he'd wanted her to come and have Christmas with his parents. With the move, he couldn't miss the family Christmas, but had wanted to spend it with her too.

"That's okay," she said softly. "I'll spend mine here crying."

She swung her legs out of the car and hauled herself to her feet, then locked up the car and headed for the house. She kept her focus on each step, using it to push away her urge to crumple into a ball and weep.

Cleo was surprisingly happy to see her, purring and weaving around her ankles instead of her usual chorus of yowling her discontent about being left when she wanted company. Scarlett bent and rubbed the cat's head. "I don't know how your evening was," she said. "But it had to be better than mine."

Scarlett changed into yoga pants and a T-shirt that sported a faded image of a disgruntled cat. The shirt had been a Christmas gift years ago from a colleague in New York.

Cleo watched Scarlett's transformation from a spot at the end of the bed. As soon as she was in comfy clothes, Scarlett scooped up the cat and carried her out to the sofa. "I can't go to bed yet," she said. "Luke is coming over."

Cleo butted her head against Scarlett's chin and cranked her purr up a notch. "Yeah, I like Luke a lot too," Scarlett said, blinking away tears. She cleared her throat. "Let's talk about something different."

Scarlett settled on the sofa with her legs curled under her. "The party was horrific," she told her cat. "Though I did see shrimp on the refreshment table. I'm sorry I didn't think to snag you a couple. I know how much you enjoy shrimp."

Cleo didn't respond to that as she'd already fallen asleep. "Good plan," Scarlett said. She snuggled into the corner of the sofa. "I'll rest my eyes for a second too."

***

Loud knocking on the front door jolted Scarlett awake, making her dump Cleo on the floor as she shot to her feet. "Sorry about that," she told the cat as she circled the sofa to head for the front door.

She pulled open the door. Luke leaned against the entryway, his bow tie hanging loose and his hair wild as if he'd been running his hands through the strands. He gave her a crooked grin, slightly less bright than usual. "You locked up the car. I thought you might leave the keys in it."

"Sorry. What time is it?" Scarlett asked.

"Late," he said. "It's tomorrow already."

"Then you probably shouldn't be driving. I'm not even sure I was safe. I was so tired. Come on in, you can spend the night in my guest room. I might even have a pair of sweats you can borrow to sleep in."

He gave a big yawn. "Much as I appreciate the offer, nothing sounds better than my own bed right now. I don't live that far away. I'm going to go ahead and go home. I'll text you when I get there so you know I made it okay."

"If you're sure." She retrieved his keys from the kitchen counter. As tired as she was, she was glad that she'd left the keys somewhere out in the open. She didn't trust herself to remember anywhere else she might have put them.

She followed him out to the car, stifling the urge to ask him about the transfer to Virginia. He'd tell her when he was ready, but she wanted him to be ready on her schedule.

"Thanks for letting me borrow the car," she said.

"Happy to oblige. You were obviously wiped out." He kissed her cheek and climbed into the Volvo. "I love you."

"I love you too." She watched him back out of the drive, turn around, and head down the street. She continued to watch until the vehicle rounded a corner out of sight. Then she walked back into the house, locked the door, and continued toward her bedroom.

Cleo fell into line behind her. "I'm about dead on my feet. Ready for bed, Cleo?" The cat meowed. Scarlett couldn't help but smile as she climbed into her bed. At least she and Cleo were always on the same page.

She placed her fingertips to her cheek where Luke had kissed her before he'd left. Tears burned her eyes. How many more kisses would she get before the final kiss goodbye?

11

Exhaustion dragged Scarlett into a confused and troubled sleep almost as soon as her head touched the pillow. She woke to the smell of fresh coffee and bacon. Cleo was gone, having been lured away by the amazing scent, no doubt. Spotting the clock beside the bed, she gasped. She'd forgotten to set the alarm and overslept church.

Scarlett sat up and stretched, surprised by how much better she felt. She had a vague recollection of dark dreams spent running through the museum as it transformed into a maze, but she wasn't sure whether she'd been running to something or away from something. "Doesn't matter," she muttered. "Dreams are weird."

Wondering if the source of the coffee and bacon aroma was Luke—who knew where her hide-a-key was—Scarlett decided to jump into the shower before facing him. She felt sure that seeing her sleep hair would not be helpful in convincing him not to move to Virginia. That thought froze her in place. *When did I decide to try to convince him not to take a promotion at work?* She wasn't sure. She wasn't even sure it was fair to Luke to try to keep him if he wanted to go, but tears threatened every time she even thought about him leaving.

The shower restored a little of her sanity. Luke's decision was Luke's decision. She'd simply wait to hear about the promotion and whether he was leaving. She was an adult. She could handle it.

She pulled on a worn pair of jeans and a light cotton sweater, then padded to the kitchen in bare feet. Luke stood at the stove in jeans and a T-shirt with *FBI* printed on it. His grin was welcoming as he held up a pan full of fluffy scrambled eggs. "Perfect timing."

"It smells fantastic," Scarlett said.

"Sorry to let myself in this morning. You weren't answering your phone and I needed to know if you were okay. When I got here and all was quiet, I figured you were still asleep, so I decided to make you breakfast. I hope it's okay that I was poking around in your kitchen."

She recalled her sneaky peek at his private letter. "No need to apologize," she said. "And you didn't need to make breakfast."

"I beg to differ," he said. "I very much needed to make breakfast. I woke up starving. We were so busy last night, and I never did get more than a couple appetizers."

"That could have been a good thing," Scarlett suggested, "in light of the coffee."

"Hopefully the kid would have fessed up if he'd sprinkled something over the food when he was done contaminating the coffee."

"Hopefully."

They settled on stools at the kitchen counter and dug into the amazing breakfast Luke had made. Though it was simple, consisting of toast, bacon, and eggs, each bite tasted perfect. "This is amazing," Scarlett said.

"Thanks. Breakfast I can do," he said. "Which is why I sometimes eat it for dinner."

Scarlett laughed. "You sound like my dad. He's amazing at breakfast, but he's pretty much relegated to chef's assistant for all the other meals."

"Not a bad place to be."

They chatted lightly about family and cooking traditions while Scarlett waited for Luke to steer the conversation around to his promotion. Instead, he changed the subject to the murder.

"I don't suppose you solved the murder in your sleep?" he asked.

Scarlett grunted. "If I did, I don't remember it. All I remember is running through the museum all night. I'm surprised I'm not even more tired this morning than I was when I went to bed."

"I don't remember my dreams at all," he said. "I crashed immediately. But today is a new day with clear heads."

Scarlett couldn't promise a clear head. Hers was full of worry about him moving across the country—something that she couldn't talk about without confessing to snooping in Luke's car. "At least we know the murderer must be part of a relatively small group—the people at the museum and Myers."

"Maybe," Luke said. "But Val has confessed that he accepted money to run errands for someone who might be the killer. We don't know that he told us about all of those errands. After all, we didn't see the note."

"He didn't find it after I left?" Scarlett wasn't surprised, but it was admittedly a setback.

Luke shook his head. "I have no idea what it said. Maybe Val opened the door for a killer as well as for Myers."

"Unless Myers and the killer are one and the same." Then she shook her head. "Though I can't imagine how Myers could have gotten into the special exhibit room. I'm absolutely certain that no one opened the door after we walked in. I was distracted by my speech, but I would have noticed a sudden burst of light flooding in. The special exhibit room, even when lit, is much darker than the second-floor landing."

"Maybe Val let the killer in much earlier," Luke said. "And the killer waited in the exhibit room."

Scarlett mulled that over. Val had admitted going into the special exhibit room himself. Maybe his story of being curious was a lie. Maybe he'd seen the inside because he'd helped the murderer sneak in there.

"If that's the case, Val could be in danger. If the killer broke into Val's apartment and stole the letter to remove evidence—and I assume we're working on that belief—then eliminating Val would also be wise because it will stop him from giving us the information we need to catch the killer."

"I thought of that last night," Luke said. "The chief is going to put an officer on the task of keeping an eye on Val and his sister."

"His sister?" Scarlett said. "That's right. He said he lives with her. She would be the one who has the second bedroom." She winced. "She must have been unhappy to come home to that mess."

"No doubt," Luke said.

Scarlett took a bite of eggs and chewed thoughtfully. "It could be even simpler. If the killer was already in the museum, they could have gone into the exhibit with us. Libby, for instance. I didn't count heads and I was focused on my speech. I'm not sure I would have noticed. I would have when my speech was over and I started interacting with everyone, but that's when the lights went out."

"I'm not sure I would have noticed either," Luke admitted. "My attention was on you."

Something in the way he said that made her smile, then she felt a fresh pang of loss. He could be leaving her. She tamped down the feeling. "We should ask everyone else there. Maybe one of them noticed someone tagging along. If it was Libby, it may not have struck anyone as odd."

"You want to start this questioning today?" Luke asked.

Scarlett's glance darted to the clock on the kitchen wall and she sighed. "Well, we missed church, so we could. I feel badly about that. It's almost Christmas. That isn't the best time to skip church."

Luke reached over and squeezed her hand. "I am sure God and Pastor Coleman won't hold it against us. Especially after last night." He shifted on the stool to study her. "Scarlett, are you happy in Crescent Harbor? I know it's different from New York, and you've had more than your share of bumps since you took the job at the museum. But are you happy?"

"This place has been more exciting than I expected at times," Scarlett said. "But yes, I love it here. I love the people I've met here. I can't imagine being anywhere else. Crescent Harbor is home now." Then she risked a question, feeling it was only fair since he'd brought up the topic. "Why do you ask? Are you happy here?"

He grinned. "I am glad you're at home here. It's been a lot, all the things you've had to deal with."

"But that's how life is," Scarlett said. "Challenging, but full of wonderful things too. I love so much here, and so many things have changed me for the better." Then she tried fishing again. "I did worry when I was offered the job. I mean, it sounded great, but sometimes something can sound good, and then flip your life upside down."

"But it proved to be the right plan," he said. "Didn't it?"

"It did," she said, suddenly afraid she'd helped in the wrong direction. Was Luke going to use her happiness as a reason to take the promotion and move to the other side of the country?

She tensed, waiting for him to admit to the promotion, but instead he crunched on his bacon before suggesting they should follow her plan. "We can check on all the people from last night. After all, it would make perfect sense for you to be concerned about them since they had come to your party."

Scarlett winced. "Thanks for the reminder that last night was my idea."

"I am not blaming you." Again he squeezed her hand. "I do think the party guests will be more inclined to share things with you that they wouldn't share with Chief Rodriguez."

"You're not trying to say you want me to do this on my own, are you?"

"No. I do not want that. But I'll be there as Scarlett McCormick's supportive boyfriend, not as an FBI agent."

"I'll give it a try," Scarlett said. Besides, the more time they spent together, the more chance Luke would spill the beans on the promotion, and then they could finally talk about it. "I do have to be at the museum at three so Libby can pick up her catering things."

"Right, and I need to drop the urn off for testing. Let's plan to visit the guests, then go about our separate chores. Where should we start?"

Scarlett considered the guests at the event. She didn't for a moment believe Allie, Greta, or Hal were involved. She could easily call them or wait until Monday to ask questions, so that left Maya and the Milstons. Since Scarlett couldn't imagine Maya plotting some cold-blooded murder—or hurting anyone at all, really—she quickly settled on the Milstons.

"I can imagine Rupert Milston planning something like this," Scarlett said. "He's probably as much of a hothead as Myers Portland. He strikes me as ruthless, and his wife acts almost afraid of him sometimes. She was particularly on edge at the event. I thought she was acting jealous of Tasha, but maybe her edginess was because she suspected Rupert was up to something."

"Can you think of a motive?" Luke asked.

"I can't think of a motive for anyone except maybe Myers," Scarlett admitted. "I don't really know the Milstons. I've talked to both of them a number of times, but always in a professional context and always connected to the museum."

Luke pondered the information. "I think your reasoning is sound. Let's go talk to the Milstons."

"Sure," Scarlett said. "I need to put shoes on and maybe tidy up in here."

"And I need to run home and change into something more presentable."

Scarlett had to agree. His casual attire wouldn't do for a visit to the Milstons. Then she considered her own well-worn jeans. They probably wouldn't either. Time for a change.

The Milstons lived in a walled community, which meant Scarlett and Luke had to talk their way past a security guard at the gate. The conversation was short-lived and ended with Luke's FBI credentials and a quick, respectful response from the guard. He even told them exactly how to weave their way through the collection of mansions to find the one belonging to the Milstons.

As they drove through the clean, quiet streets of the community, Scarlett shuddered at the excess all around her. Every house struck her as entirely too big for anyone's needs. Some of the homes were nearly as big as the museum, and when they finally reached the Milstons' house, the farthest from the gate, she realized theirs was the biggest home of all.

The sprawling house had a circular drive up to the front door with a paved parking area off to one side. Luke left his car there.

"I can't imagine living this way," Scarlett said as they approached the ornate front door.

"It's not my dream home either," he said.

Scarlett sent him a questioning glance. "What *is* your dream home? The house you have is adorable."

Luke laughed. "That's exactly what every guy hopes for. An adorable house."

"It's adorable in a manly way," Scarlett assured him.

They were still smiling when the housekeeper answered the door and let them in. "Mrs. Milston is waiting for you in the sitting room."

"She knew we were coming?" Scarlett asked.

"The gate guard called," the housekeeper said, dropping her voice. "He has to. He'd get fired if he let someone show up with no warning."

"No problem," Luke said.

The housekeeper led them the long way to the sitting room, making Scarlett wonder again why anyone would want to live in such a massive place. The interior of the house was lovely with the kind of modern crispness that tended to come from a professional decorator.

Finally the housekeeper opened a set of French doors that led into a large room. Angelique was rather artfully settled on a settee with the draping folds of her long silk dressing gown arranged far too perfectly to be natural. Had the poor woman been fussing with her clothes while they wandered?

If so, she spoiled the perfect arrangement by getting gracefully to her feet. "Sorry to greet you in this condition. I slept in after the horrible strain of last night. We were awakened by the call saying you were on your way to the house."

"Sorry to put you to that trouble," Scarlett replied, though she couldn't help noticing Angelique's hair and makeup were as perfect as the folds of her gown had been. Everything about the scene felt like theater. "Will your husband be joining us?"

"Yes, any minute now," Angelique said. "I assume you've stopped by to tell us the police have arrested Tasha's ex."

"Oh?" Luke said as if the thought had never occurred to him. "I wasn't aware he was in the special exhibit room with all of us when Mrs. Portland died. Did you see him there?"

"No, of course not. I was focused on Scarlett and her lovely speech. I had been looking forward to the evening for a week. It's such a shame it was all ruined." She brushed at a nonexistent speck of dust on her gown, then gestured toward the sofa. "I suppose you should sit if we're going to have an interrogation."

"No interrogation." Scarlett approached the sofa warily. It was a unique piece, almost sculptural in its design, and she doubted it was comfortable. She sat on a cushion and winced. She'd underestimated how uncomfortable it would be. "We're simply visiting guests who were at the party last night to see if everyone is all right."

Luke took the spot beside her. He didn't make a face but his body language reflected the stiffness of the piece of furniture. "And to hear anything you've remembered since last night," he said. "Sometimes after the shock of an event fades, small details come to mind."

"I have no desire to rehash that awful night," Angelique said.

"Yes," Scarlett agreed. "It was especially awful for poor Tasha. So you didn't see anything out of the ordinary in the exhibit room?"

"I barely saw anything at all," Angelique said. "As you well know, the lights went out. But really, the killer must have been Myers. He was bold enough, surely, after barging into the event and ranting at poor Tasha."

"How well did you know Mrs. Portland?" Luke asked.

Angelique waved her hand, showing off a flawless manicure and making Scarlett think again about the theater of the whole conversation. "I barely knew her at all. We ran in the same circles. Crescent Harbor isn't large, and there are so few of our social standing. But we weren't chums."

"Did Mrs. Portland live in this community?" Luke asked. "It certainly appears to be large enough."

Angelique wrinkled her nose. "No. I don't think this is Tasha's style. She once said something terribly rude about gated communities, as if wanting a certain level of security made us all cowards. She did love wearing the renegade facade, brave and daring."

"You disapproved of her," Luke observed.

"I never said that," Angelique insisted. "I had no particular feeling about her one way or another. I suppose I felt sorry for her, with all the unpleasantness of a divorce. I can't imagine anything worse. It reminds me to be grateful for my own marriage every day."

Scarlett studied the other woman, suspecting she was lying. But about how much? She disliked Tasha, but Scarlett had suspected that at the event. And Scarlett wondered how sound Angelique and Rupert's marriage was. He'd acted uninterested and even annoyed with her the night before, at least until they closed ranks after the murder.

There were so many undercurrents that Scarlett couldn't sort them out. One thing she knew for sure was that nothing about the situation could be taken at face value. Angelique was working hard to convince Luke and Scarlett of something, and that meant she was afraid they were going to figure out the truth—whatever that was. All they had to do was uncover the secret.

Sure. How hard could that be?

12

"It wasn't as if I didn't try to be friends with Tasha." Angelique leaned toward them as if trying to drive the words forward with her posture and make them believe her insistent tone. "But I soon realized it wasn't going to work."

"Why is that?" Scarlett asked.

"She wasn't particularly friendly. She could pretend all right when it suited her, but everything was always about her. And she could be positively nasty when she chose to."

"I hadn't noticed that about her."

Angelique pursed her lips. "Lucky you. She constantly reminded me that I'm a handful of years older than her, as if that makes any difference at all. There were times I thought I'd scream or knock her down." Then she froze, realizing what she'd said.

"Don't worry about it," Scarlett said. "If we were guilty of everything we said in jest, the population of the world would be radically reduced."

"Do you know of anyone else who was a frequent target of Tasha's nasty remarks?" Luke asked.

"I never paid attention. I don't understand this line of questioning anyway."

"The more we know, the quicker we can find the killer," Luke explained.

Angelique wrinkled her forehead. "We?"

"I *am* FBI," Luke reminded her.

"Right. Well, obviously, there was only one person who could have done this," Angelique insisted as she fiddled with the edge of her dressing gown. "It was Myers. If the police haven't arrested him, then I seriously question their competence."

"Have you ever seen Myers Portland behave violently toward Tasha?" Scarlett asked.

"No," the other woman admitted. "But we all knew what a hothead he could be. I once heard him ranting about a sports team. Can you imagine? Who would waste energy on something so inane? A lunatic, I tell you."

Luke laughed, a sound he quickly covered with a cough. "Actually I've probably ranted about sports a time or two myself. Sports fans can be passionate. Do you have a more relevant example?"

Angelique shifted on the settee, obviously upset that they weren't simply accepting what she was trying to say. Scarlett wondered more and more why she was trying so hard to keep their attention on Myers. "I can't believe you have any doubt," Angelique said. "You saw him at the party, the same as the rest of us. The man is unhinged."

"I did," Luke agreed. "I also saw him leave. And I did not see him enter the exhibit with us."

"That doesn't mean he didn't," Angelique said sulkily.

No one spoke for a long moment, giving Angelique time to stew. She continued to arrange and rearrange the folds of her dressing gown. Scarlett thought back to the night of the party and how Angelique's husband had cut her off several times when she spoke. Why was he leaving her to deal with them alone?

"Where is Rupert?" Scarlett asked.

Angelique waved away the question. "Getting dressed, I suppose. People who say women take forever to get ready have never met my husband. He won't be down until he looks perfect."

Scarlett considered the obvious care Angelique had taken with her hair and makeup, but decided not to mention it. "Does he know you're chatting with us?"

"I am not responsible for what Rupert does or does not know."

"Do you know how he felt about Tasha?" Luke asked.

That question must have caught Angelique off guard, because she froze for an instant before answering without meeting Luke's eyes. "I doubt he thought about her one way or another. I don't believe he ever cared for Myers, which meant we never invited them over for anything but large social gatherings."

"He acted interested in chatting with her at the party last night," Scarlett said. "In fact, he walked off while I was talking to you and went straight to Tasha."

"Probably something business-related. Tasha was always far more interested in business than I am. I focus on the arts and bettering our community."

"Tasha donated generously to the museum," Scarlett pointed out. "So she must have been interested in the arts too."

"Or she enjoyed having you fawn over her for giving a few dollars."

Scarlett was surprised by the snippy remark. Angelique was coming to the end of her willingness to be polite. Sometimes a burst of temper revealed even more interesting things than grudging politeness.

"What kind of business would Tasha and your husband have been doing?" Luke asked.

Angelique threw her hands in the air. "How would I know? It probably wasn't about the museum. Rupert has virtually no interest in that at all. Our charitable giving is really him indulging me. Tasha fancied herself a real estate mogul, so I imagine it had something to do with that."

"But you're sure it was business?" Luke pushed further. "Not personal?"

"There was nothing personal between them," Angelique snapped.

A deep voice sounded from the doorway. "I wouldn't say nothing. I rather admired Tasha. She was an intelligent and vibrant woman."

Angelique responded to that as if Rupert had smacked her. She raised a palm to her cheek and stared wide-eyed at him, but didn't say a word.

As Angelique had told them to expect, Rupert was positively dapper in tailored slacks with creases so sharp they looked dangerous. With them he wore a white shirt with several of the top buttons undone and the sleeves neatly rolled.

"Were you talking business with her at the party?" Luke asked him.

"After a fashion," Rupert said. "I was telling her I planned to sue her father."

That sent a shock around the room. Scarlett had not expected information like that to come to light.

Fortunately, Luke was far less thrown off by it. "Why is that?" he asked, his tone even.

Rupert snorted. "Tasha's father is Adrian Belsky."

Luke merely nodded.

"As an FBI agent, you probably know the man is ruthless and unscrupulous."

"Not exactly rare traits in an extremely wealthy businessman," Luke said.

"Perhaps not, but Adrian lured me into a bad business deal that was nearly disastrous for my business. When I demanded he make reparations for the damage he'd done, he laughed and told me that was the point of the deal."

"I don't understand," Scarlett said.

Rupert gave her a condescending look. "He saw me as competition and wanted me out of business."

"But your business survived," Scarlett said. She had to assume it had considering they'd recently given a generous donation to the museum.

"Naturally." Rupert smirked. "Adrian underestimated how careful I am about my business actions. Trusting him was a serious miscalculation, but I also plan for possible failure of any deal. I've had years of experience swimming in shark-infested waters."

"What did any of that have to do with Tasha?" Scarlett asked.

"There are few things in the world that Adrian Belsky cares about," Rupert said. "Tasha was one. I hoped she'd be able to talk him into making good on what he'd done. If I sue, it will be messy and public. Something like that is delicate, because the wrong public perception of my business could do as much damage as the bad deal did."

"Did Tasha say she'd do something about it?" Scarlett asked.

"No." Rupert's face darkened. "But she was distracted all evening. In light of what happened with Myers, I have to assume her preoccupation had to do with him. Normally, she's much more receptive to what I have to say."

"Yes, *receptive*," Angelique snarled. The woman's face registered revulsion toward her husband.

"You have a vivid imagination," Rupert said, his own expression cold and blank. "As I have told you many times."

Angelique didn't respond to the rebuke.

"As much as I enjoy airing our temporary marital bump in front of near strangers," Rupert said. "I need to drive into the office, and I know you have things to do as well, Angelique." He smiled, though nothing in his eyes showed the slightest joy. "I'm afraid I'm going to have to ask you both to leave so we can get on with our day."

Luke rose. "I'm glad to see you both weathered last night's events well enough."

"It was horrible," Angelique insisted.

"It was certainly tragic," Rupert said. "I'm sorry for Tasha, but it has nothing to do with us. We didn't see anything that you didn't see.

After all, as an FBI agent you're a trained observer."

"I am," Luke agreed. "Thank you for your time."

"I'll call for the housekeeper to show you out," Angelique said, popping to her feet.

"Not necessary," Luke said. "I memorized the way. You know, as a trained observer."

Rupert laughed at that and his expression became fractionally warmer. "Then I'm sure you'll both make it out of here unscathed."

Luke put his arm around Scarlett and guided her out of the room past Rupert. As Scarlett passed the man, she had a pang of unease. She'd spoken with Rupert on a number of occasions, but never before had she recognized the almost predatory air he could assume. It was distinctly discomforting.

Once they were out of the grand house and heading for the car, Luke asked Scarlett what she thought of the Milstons.

"I'm not sure what to think. I find him reptilian, which I've never considered before. Angelique has always been sulky, but I didn't realize they had problems between them. I wonder what the story is there."

They reached the car, and Luke opened the door for her. "Can you think of anyone who might know and be willing to share that knowledge with us?"

Scarlett shook her head as she climbed inside. "I'm starting to realize that I don't know any of the guests well, other than Allie and the Barons."

"I think we're safe in assuming those three aren't killers." Luke closed the door and walked around to the driver's side.

Scarlett relaxed into the seat and thought again of the deep, cold undercurrents she'd sensed in every moment Angelique and Rupert were together. Something was wrong with the couple, and Angelique had been upset when Rupert went to speak to Tasha at the party. Why would she care if Rupert was merely interested in discussing business?

Luke opened the driver's side door and got in, resuming the conversation. "I'm going to find out more about this business deal between Rupert and Tasha's father."

"I suspect Rupert hates him," Scarlett said. "But I don't see how that could have led to Tasha's death."

Luke started the car. "Sometimes the paths to murder are convoluted."

"True," she agreed. "But if Tasha wasn't involved in the business deal, it is an unlikely connection. I am interested in what Angelique said about Tasha needling people."

"You think someone killed her for being passive aggressive?" Luke asked.

"No, but if Tasha was needling Angelique about being old, she clearly enjoyed getting Angelique's goat. Maybe Tasha hinted that she was after Rupert now that she was single again. I got the impression at the party that Angelique was jealous. Maybe she thought Tasha was trying to steal her husband."

"I've heard worse motives for murder," Luke said.

"So a bad business deal or a jealous spouse. We picked up two suspects, but no real answers."

"There is no reason to focus on the Milstons yet," Luke said. "But I wouldn't be comfortable with ignoring them either. They both had access to Tasha in the dark. I'm going to put my people on finding out more about this business with Rupert and Adrian Belsky. That and the contents of the urn are my main interests at present."

"And I want to know more about Angelique and Tasha, but we may be on our way to the very place to learn that. Maya is part of their social crowd—maybe not a close part, but close enough to provide some insight."

"What do you know about Maya?" Luke asked. "I'm not sure I exchanged words with her last night."

"She's shy, I think," Scarlett said. "But I often find the quietest people have the deepest insights into others. They hear more because they aren't waiting for their time to talk."

Luke paused at the guardhouse. "Can you give me Maya's address?"

"Sure." Scarlett read off the address from her contacts and felt a strange relief once they'd passed out of the gated community. She knew the walls and gates were there to keep people out, but they reminded her too much of prisons. She shuddered at the thought.

"You okay?" Luke asked.

"Gated communities creep me out," she said. "It's nothing."

"I'm not a fan either," he admitted. "They make for great places to hide. Hide from the outside world and hide secrets as well."

Scarlett twisted to peer at the walls receding in the distance as they drove. What secrets were hiding in there? Had they led to murder?

13

As they approached Maya's house, Scarlett marveled at how much it was the exact opposite of the Milstons' home. Maya didn't live in a gated community, but in an almost blindingly white modern home perched on the edge of the cliffs overlooking the ocean.

When they got out of the car, Scarlett could hear the pounding of the surf against the rocks far below. "This place is really something."

"I prefer my place," he said. "My job is death-defying enough. I don't need my house to be as well."

Scarlett took the lead near the front door, which was a light wood surrounded by panels of glass. She pressed the button beside the door and heard chimes tinkling inside.

The door opened almost immediately. Maya stared out at them with no clear expression on her face. "Welcome," she said. "Won't you come in?"

The slender woman wore a pale silk pantsuit with a long jacket that matched her home. The suit was impeccably tailored, making Scarlett wonder if it had been made especially for Maya. Wealth showed itself in so many ways. The expensive silk suit was offset by Maya's bare feet.

"Should we take off our shoes?" Scarlett asked as they stepped through the door.

Maya shook her head. "No, you're fine. I enjoy the feeling of the floor under my feet. I have no problem with shoes in my house."

Maya led them to the large open living area where tall windows offered breathtaking views of the ocean. Despite the modern design, Maya had managed to make it both interesting and cozy with an eclectic mix of styles and patterns, including mismatched rugs layered over one another to warm up the marble floors.

"Please sit." Maya waved toward an overstuffed sofa. "Can I get you anything? Tea perhaps?"

"We're fine," Luke said.

"As you wish." Maya settled into a pale-blue chair, curling her bare feet under her. "What brings you to my home today? I love visitors, but I believe this is a first for you, Scarlett."

"It is," Scarlett admitted. "Your home is lovely, though I'd be terrified of living on the side of a cliff. Don't you worry about earthquakes?"

"This home was designed by a Japanese architect with experience in earthquake country. The build employs all the most modern protection techniques. I know that humans can do only so much against the vagaries of nature, but I couldn't imagine living anywhere else."

"You have an amazing view," Luke said.

"I do," Maya agreed. "Have you come to bring me permission to retrieve my painting?"

Scarlett was surprised by the question. "The police work as fast as they can, but I wouldn't expect the crime scene to be released this soon."

"No one," Luke said, "not even Scarlett, will be allowed into the exhibit for the next several days at least."

"I cannot even check on my painting?" Maya asked.

Luke shook his head. "But the police are aware of the value of the contents of that room. They won't be careless."

"But they won't know how fragile things can be," Maya protested. "Fingerprint powder and other intrusive methods could damage my painting."

"Your painting is under glass," Scarlett said, not wanting to argue, but confused by how upset Maya was. "Fingerprint powder couldn't even touch it."

"The handmade frame isn't under glass," Maya snapped. Then she paused, took a deep breath, and visibly calmed. "I'm sorry for my outburst. I know this is trying for you as well. I'm overly emotional because that painting was the focal point of my late father's art collection. The rest of his collection was sold to pay off his debts when he died, but I managed to keep that one. It is my connection to him."

"I understand," Scarlett said.

"Do you? The young woman stepping away from her frowning father in the painting reminds me of my own life. My father didn't approve of my interest in business over marriage and children. He expected me to carry on his lineage, and instead I went my own way."

"That must have been difficult," Scarlett said.

"At first," Maya agreed. "But once my father saw that business was truly my passion, we reconciled. I consider that the mark of a great man, the ability to change. The painting reminds me that the past does not define the future."

"Was your father a businessman as well?" Luke asked. "You mentioned debts."

"My father was an architect. He taught me to appreciate the art that goes into the creation of a building, a lesson I brought to choosing an architect for my home."

"And yet, he ended up in debt," Luke said. Scarlett fought the urge to frown at him. Did he not realize the topic was a sore one for Maya?

"He was a fine architect," Maya insisted. "But he was an utterly dreadful businessman. If we had reconciled sooner than we did, I could have helped him. By the time he showed me the depth of the problem, it was severe. But we were working on it when he died unexpectedly." She blinked rapidly, but otherwise she maintained her eerie calm.

"At least you had a chance to reconcile," Scarlett said.

"I am grateful for that." Maya cleared her throat. "You have actually seen some of my father's work quite closely, Scarlett."

"Oh?"

"Yes. He designed the addition to the first floor of the museum after Devon Reed bought the property. You must have noticed how perfectly it blended with the old building? That was my father's doing."

"It's amazing," Scarlett said.

Maya beamed at her. "It was not an easy task since the new additions have so many more windows, but my father was astonishing. He and Devon were quite close, which is why I donate regularly to the museum, and why I agreed to loan the painting my father loved."

"I'm grateful for the loan," Scarlett said. "It inspired some of my other choices, but I completely understand your desire to have the painting home safe and sound, even though it will be gravely missed."

Maya merely nodded. Scarlett had hoped Maya would relent after some time to think about it, but she was beginning to realize that would not happen. She would need to find a new piece to fill that spot in the exhibit.

"Miss Shepherd," Luke said, "what did you think of Tasha Portland?"

"I thought of her very little at all," Maya replied. "We ran into one another. Crescent Harbor can be a small town that way, but I often find socializing with people who hold great wealth to be trying. Most of my friends are not from among that group."

"So you disliked her," Luke said.

Maya chuckled. "I did not put nearly that much energy into it. I found Tasha rather pushy, but she was fine otherwise. She was still a child in many ways. I understand she was overindulged by her parents, and it left her horribly self-absorbed and entitled. But, as I said, she struck me as a child in a woman's body, and one doesn't blame a child for being a child."

"That's an interesting way to think about it," Luke said. "Did you know Tasha's parents?"

"I know of them," Maya said. "Her father is a real force in the business world, and I know he continued to support her, though I heard that her mother wasn't always in favor of spoiling Tasha quite so much."

Scarlett thought Maya knew rather a lot about Tasha, considering she'd claimed to have paid Tasha scant attention. "At least you and Tasha shared an interest in art," Scarlett said. "Tasha also donated regularly to the museum."

Maya shook her head. "Tasha saw art as decoration. I believe art holds the soul of humanity. That may have been the biggest difference between us. There is one thing I admired about Tasha, though."

"What was that?" Scarlett said. She'd begun to think Maya's feelings for Tasha were stronger than she cared to let on.

"She refused to take her husband back after he'd left in a fit of temper," Maya said. "That took courage."

Scarlett had felt Luke perk up as Maya spoke, so she wasn't surprised when he asked the next question. "Do you know what provoked the fight that made him leave?"

"Yes, she told me. She said she'd refused to finance some project he wanted. She complained that Myers treated her more like a bank than a wife."

"So his finances would have taken a hit with the divorce," Scarlett said.

"I suppose. I haven't spoken to him since then, or even seen him other than that embarrassing display last night. I assume he is the chief suspect in Tasha's murder. He's definitely the most obvious one."

"The police are investigating everyone with a possible motive," Luke said noncommittally.

"Maya, how well do you know the Milstons?" Scarlett asked.

Maya shrugged. "I know them well enough to exchange friendly words, but I wouldn't say we're close or anything. I do like Angelique, but the couple is ill-matched."

"What do you mean by that?" Scarlett asked.

"Angelique needs a lot of reassurance and simple affection. Rupert isn't particularly good at either." Maya shook her head slowly. "Poor Angelique. She worries constantly that Rupert is going to trade her in for a younger model, though I think her worry is for nothing."

"Why is that?" Scarlett asked. "He does act rather cold toward her."

"Rupert is cold by nature," Maya said, "which is something Angelique is not able to see. It would be different if he were warm and welcoming to everyone but her, but he isn't. She even told me that she thought Rupert was considering leaving her for Tasha. I still believe that notion was absurd. I don't think Rupert would trade in one needy wife for another simply because the new one was younger, but Angelique was convinced of it." She smoothed her pant leg. "I suppose that kind of behavior is common in our socioeconomic group, husbands trading in wives as if they're used cars."

"Did you ever get the feeling Angelique was afraid of Rupert?" Scarlett asked.

Maya raised her elegant eyebrows. "Do you mean physically afraid?" She laughed, then held up a hand. "I'm sorry. It was rude of me to laugh. No, I don't think she's afraid of Rupert. That kind of behavior requires a level of passion he doesn't have, at least not for anything outside of business. He can be verbally unkind, and I expect he ignores her a good deal, but I would say without hesitation that he wouldn't cause her physical harm."

"You sound sure," Luke said.

"I am. He indulges her whims," she said. "He has no interest in the museum, for example. That's all Angelique. And yet I know they donate generously. I think Rupert is fond of Angelique, or at least as fond as he's capable of. I don't know him well socially, but we've crossed swords in business. And I hear gossip, even if I'd prefer to avoid it."

"Thank you for your candor about all of our questions," Scarlett said.

"As I said, I hear gossip," Maya said. "Including gossip about your inability to ignore a puzzle. I assume anything you learn will help the police with this investigation, and I'm all for anything that helps the police. The sooner they have answers and release your special exhibit room, the sooner I get my painting home safely. So my motives are entirely selfish."

"I still appreciate it."

Maya inclined her head. "Now I'm curious. Who do you think killed Tasha?"

"I honestly don't know," Scarlett said. "I'm learning there were a lot of things going on behind the scenes that I knew nothing about."

"Who do you think killed Tasha?" Luke asked.

Maya didn't answer immediately, her expression pensive. Finally she said, "If it were not so logistically difficult, I would feel certain it was Myers. He is an emotional time bomb. But I have not been able to determine how he could have gotten into the room. My next candidate would be Angelique since she'd developed quite a loathing for Tasha, but I don't think Angelique has it in her to murder anyone. All in all, I am glad I am not the policeman tasked with figuring this out."

"I think I am too." Scarlett rose from the sofa, and Maya matched her action, though with considerably more fluid grace. "Luke and I should be going. Again, thank you for answering our questions. And I enjoyed seeing your beautiful home."

"Do come again under more pleasant circumstances," Maya said. "This house is spectacular in a storm."

"I don't think I have that kind of nerve," Scarlett said. She clasped hands briefly with Maya, then she and Luke left. Once they were outside, Scarlett felt the warmth of Luke's hand in hers. "That was interesting."

"It was," Luke said as they crossed a bed of white gravel that made up the parking area. "I don't think we gained any new suspects, though I suppose the motives of the ones we had have deepened somewhat."

Once in the car, Luke waited until Scarlett was buckled in to say, "I'll drive you over to the museum. I want to check out the special exhibit room before I leave you."

Scarlett gaped at him. "Is that even allowed?"

"I'm FBI," he said. "I'll call the chief before I cross the barrier. The techs have undoubtedly come and gone."

"Then why haven't they released the scene yet?" Scarlett asked.

"Because sometimes the things they discover in the first pass send them back for another search," he said. "But I still think the chief won't mind me examining the crime scene."

"In that case, can you ask if I can peek over your shoulder?" she asked.

He grinned. "That, my dear, is a given."

As they approached the Reed Museum of Art and Archaeology several minutes later, it struck Scarlet that the parking lot was rarely empty, even when she left at the end of her workday. Driving across the lot with no cars to avoid felt strange. The few security staff were parked close to the building, something they couldn't do when the museum was open and prime parking was reserved for guests.

Scarlett unlocked the front door and they walked in. "I need to scare up one of the security people to watch this door. Libby isn't due to arrive for a while, but I'll need someone here to let her in."

"I need to make my calls to the chief," Luke said, "so I can stay here while you find someone. If Libby comes early, I'll be here."

"You're such a useful boyfriend," Scarlett teased. She kissed him on the cheek and strode toward the elevator that would take her to the basement, where she'd find security personnel.

A man in the museum's security uniform met her as soon as she stepped out of the elevator. "I saw you on the video feed, Ms. McCormick," he said. "Is there anything you need?"

"You're not here alone, are you?" she asked.

He shook his head. "Mick is in the office. I popped down for a cup of coffee before my next rounds."

"Good. I need someone to come and watch the front door. The caterer from last night is coming to get her platters and such. I need someone to let her in."

"No problem."

"Thanks." They stepped into the elevator together, and she studied him. Scarlett rarely chatted with the security staff. Winnie handled all of that so well that Scarlett didn't want to make her feel as if Scarlett were trying to micromanage her work. "Were you here last night?"

"Yes ma'am. It's been the weirdest double shift ever."

"A murder will do that," she said.

"It was more than that. After everyone finally went home, we saw someone on the exterior cameras a couple times."

Scarlett stiffened. "Someone outside?"

"On the grounds, and sometimes the guy tried the doors. It was the same guy who snuck in and shouted at his ex-wife."

The elevator reached the ground floor and opened. Scarlett stepped out. "Did you call the police?"

"That's not protocol," the man said. "We call in the case of actual breaches or if someone is intent on damage outside. The protocol was set by the previous curator because people sometimes come to the museum when it's not open for the sole purpose of strolling the grounds here, and that's something Mr. Reed always wanted to encourage."

"I see." Scarlett picked up her pace, eager to reach Luke. "We may need to rethink that protocol when there's been a murder and the victim was accosted by the person wandering the grounds and trying to get inside."

"Yes ma'am."

Scarlett reached Luke ahead of the guard. "Myers Portland was outside after the murder," she told him.

"Outside here?"

"He'll be on the security feed. Apparently he even tried the doors."

Luke faced the guard as he approached. "Did you see when he left?"

The man shook his head. "He kept coming in and out of range of the cameras. He was wandering around, mostly on the seaside of the building, and he wasn't exactly steady on his feet."

"He was sick?" Scarlett asked.

"He was inebriated," the guard said.

"I think maybe we should take a quick stroll around the grounds before we head upstairs," Luke suggested.

"Do you want me to come with you?" the guard asked.

"No," Scarlett said. "Watch for the caterer, but don't let her go upstairs by herself. Keep her down here until we get back."

"Yes ma'am."

Scarlett and Luke went outside and strode around to the rear of the building. The grounds there were open with a beautifully maintained lawn and a variety of flower beds, shrubs, and small trees. It didn't leave a person much room to hide unless they cared to hug the sides of the building where palm trees, shrubs, and hedges grew.

"Do we poke through the hedges?" Scarlett asked.

"I think we should."

Scarlett wasn't a squeamish person. Archaeology required being outside in heat and rain and squeezing into spaces where small creatures like spiders thrived. Still, she couldn't help wondering what sort of things lived in the palm trees and hedges, and how many of them could end up in her clothes and hair. Luke, on the other hand, didn't act as if he gave that idea any consideration at all and pushed his way to the wall behind the plantings.

"There's a lot of space in this gap," he said. "We should walk the length of it."

"Right," Scarlett said.

They pushed through the narrow space all the way to the corner of the building before they saw anything other than leaf litter and sticks. But when they edged around the side of the building, Scarlett spotted the dark figure on the ground. Though she couldn't see the man's head, hidden as it was by one arm, she recognized the clothing at once. She'd seen the blue jeans, rumpled shirt, and blazer the night before, though all looked considerably worse for wear in the daylight.

The man on the ground was Myers Portland, and he wasn't moving.

14

Luke knelt beside the prone figure and pressed his fingers to the skin of the man's throat before bending close to his face. "His pulse is strong and he's breathing."

Scarlett realized she wasn't. She'd been holding her breath while she waited for the verdict, and she took a gulp of air as relief filled her.

"Is he hurt?" she asked. Something had to be wrong. The hard, cold ground was not where anyone would choose to spend the night.

Luke rolled Myers onto his back to see him better and discovered the man had been partially covering an empty champagne bottle, the same sort the caterer had served the night before. "My guess is either someone clonked him with this," Luke said. "Or he knocked himself out by drinking the whole thing." He leaned closer and smacked the man's cheek. "Myers? Can you hear me? Myers?"

Myers opened eyes so red they hurt to look at. He groaned. "Not so loud," he begged in a hoarse whisper. "My head is killing me."

Scarlett squatted beside Luke. "Myers, what are you doing here?"

"Keep your voice down, please." Myers struggled to sit up, and Luke helped him. "I was waiting for someone to open this place so I could find out what happened to my wife."

Scarlett winced. "You mean you don't know about Tasha?"

He began to babble, his voice growing stronger as the words poured out. "I know she was hurt. The police came by my apartment to ask about my behavior at the museum. They were asking if I hurt her, but they wouldn't tell me anything at all. How hurt is she? They wouldn't even tell me what hospital she was in. I tried calling the hospitals, but no one would tell me anything, even though I'm her husband. I knew you'd know, so I came to talk to you. What happened? Is she all right?"

"I'm sorry. She's not all right," Scarlett said as gently as she could. "She died."

He gaped at her, then burst into tears, moaning Tasha's name as he rocked. Then his eyes snapped open, suddenly far more lucid and clear. "The police thought I hurt her. That means someone hurt her. Who killed my wife?"

"We don't know," Scarlett said.

"How can you not know?" he demanded. "You were there. You must have seen them."

Luke took the man by the arm and Scarlett could tell by the way Luke's fingers sank in that his grip was tight. "We know you paid the caterer's assistant to let you into the museum. Why did you do that?"

"Not to hurt her," Myers insisted. "I would never hurt her. I loved Tasha. I loved her so much." Sobs choked his voice again.

Luke shook the man slightly. "Why did you do it?"

"I didn't do it," he moaned. "I didn't hurt her."

"Not that," Luke said, raising his voice to cut through the man's state. "Why did you pay someone to let you into the museum?"

"To talk to her," he said. "To make her see that the divorce was all wrong. We still loved each other. I knew it. Deep down, she knew it too."

"And what did you do when you were asked to leave?"

"I left," Myers insisted, then relented. "Sort of."

"How does anyone sort of leave?" Scarlett asked.

He shrugged. "I left the building, but I hung around out here for a while. I figured the party wouldn't last that long and when she came out, I'd talk to her. But then the police showed up. I thought someone had called the police about my crashing the party. I know I was out of line, but I loved her so much. I would never, ever have hurt her." He broke down into tears again.

Luke and Scarlett gave the man a few minutes to get himself under control. Finally, the sobs began to fade and Myers scrubbed at his face with his hand.

"So what did you do when the police came?" Scarlett asked.

"I went down the street and called a cab. I thought about stopping for a drink, but I'd grabbed a bottle of champagne on my way out, and I decided to go home. I figured I'd drink the champagne and go to bed."

"So you left right after the police got here?"

He bobbed his head several times. "I thought they might come out and grab me if I stayed. I saw you had cameras out here."

"How did the champagne get back here?" Scarlett asked.

He blinked at her, and she could practically see him gathering his fuzzy thoughts. "I went home, but I didn't drink the champagne. I had some beer instead. Then I came back here after I talked to the police." He squinted at the bottle. "I was out of beer, so I brought the champagne. I don't usually drink champagne much, but I think I did drink it this time. I sort of remember that. I was upset." Then he groaned, frustrated. "I don't know. I don't remember."

"That's all right," Luke said. "I'm going to call you a cab and get you home. If you remember anything after you finish sleeping this off, call me." He showed Myers his card before tucking it into the pocket of the man's blazer.

Scarlett and Luke hauled Myers to his feet. They led the man around to the front of the building and helped him sit on one of the stone benches in front of the museum while Luke called for the cab. The security man watched them from the front door and waved. Luke lifted a hand in reply.

"Once you get home, you need to stay there," Luke said. "The police may want to talk to you again. Do you have your phone?"

Myers patted his pockets and shook his head. "It's probably at my apartment."

"Did you drive here?" Scarlett asked. "Is your car in the lot?"

"No, I don't drive when I've been drinking. I took a cab."

"That's smart," Scarlett told him.

Myers eyes welled up. "I wouldn't want to hurt anyone."

Scarlett couldn't help but feel for the man. He was a wreck, and she had the impression that he didn't always make the wisest decisions, but she believed his grief. She sat beside him on the bench, and Myers grew calmer with her there, though she said nothing. Luke made a few other calls while they waited for the cab, but he had stepped away and she couldn't hear anything he said.

When the cab came, Luke and Scarlett escorted Myers to the vehicle. He was still wobbly, but capable of walking. Luke asked Myers for his address and then passed it on to the driver along with money for the fare.

"Please," Scarlett said, "make sure he gets inside okay."

"No problem," the cab driver said. He held up the cash. "It won't cost nearly this much."

"If you get him inside, consider your tip well-earned," Luke said.

The man's face lit up. "Sure, thanks. Merry Christmas."

"Merry Christmas."

The cab had barely pulled away before the catering van drove into the lot. "Libby has good timing," Luke said, inclining his head toward the entrance.

"I'll keep an eye on her if you want to go," Scarlett said.

"I think I'll stay a little longer," Luke said.

Libby pulled up to the curb and opened her door. "Can I leave this here? It'll make loading easier."

"Since the museum is closed, that should be fine," Scarlett said.

Libby hopped out. In stark contrast to Myers, Libby looked well-rested and wore jeans and a sweater in a ridiculous Christmas pattern with palm trees alternating with Santa hats. She saw Scarlett notice her sweater. "Christmas party later," she said.

"Catering or attending?" Scarlett asked as they started toward the museum doors, and Luke fell in line with them.

"Both," Libby said. "It's my sister's party. My mom is judging an ugly sweater contest."

"Good luck with that," Scarlett said.

Libby laughed. "No chance. My sister wins every year." They reached the door, and the guard opened it for them. "Can you help me load my stuff?"

"Sure," Luke said. "And we can chat."

"Lucky me," Libby said, sounding anything but happy.

"This morning we found Myers Portland outside," Scarlett said. "He had one of your champagne bottles."

"Probably snagged it from the spare case near the employee door," Libby said. "If he'd gotten it from my van, I would have noticed."

They walked the rest of the way to the second-floor landing without speaking, and Libby set to work gathering her things. "Thanks for cleaning up," she said, casting a side glance at Scarlett as Luke texted an update to the chief. "I assume you did this."

"I did. I don't care to leave food out. I'll give you your second check while you're here too. No point mailing it."

Libby's eyes widened. "I figured you were going to refuse to pay that, all things considered."

"You did your job," Scarlett said. "And Val has admitted to putting something in the coffee, so it wasn't your doing."

"That's decent of you." A true friendly smile took years off her face.

"I try to be fair," Scarlett said.

"We will have to hold your urn for a while," Luke said. "I want to know exactly what was put in the coffee."

"That's all right," Libby said. "I have a second one. It's battered, but it'll work through the holidays."

Scarlett lent a hand in packing the dishes and supplies into crates that Libby had left stacked under the long tablecloth of the refreshments table. The table itself folded up, and then Luke and Scarlett helped the caterer carry everything out to her van. Scarlett hated to be so suspicious, but she simply felt safer staying beside the woman the whole time she was in the museum.

Once Libby was gone, Luke said he was ready for a quick examination of the special exhibit room. "I'll need to head out right after so I can get that urn tested. I'll collect Myers's champagne bottle before I leave as well."

They crossed the second-floor landing on the way to the special exhibit. "When I texted the chief, I told him I'd be taking a peek in here. He wasn't as happy as he could have been, but he didn't forbid me either."

"I don't suppose you mentioned me coming in," Scarlett said.

"Actually, I said it would be helpful for you to see the room as well. Your last time in the room was interrupted by the discovery of a body, so we still don't know if any of the art was disturbed while the lights were out. If it was, it would point the investigation in a whole new direction."

"And he agreed to that?"

Luke grinned at her. "He didn't disagree."

They carefully ducked under the crime scene tape, and Luke opened the door to the exhibit room for Scarlett. Though the lights flickered on with no issues, Scarlett was still nervous as she stepped into the room. The beauty of the exhibits inside soon captivated her again. She'd never grow tired of staring at the ancient depictions of women.

They stopped at the first exhibit, and Luke pulled a flashlight out of his pocket to use as a pointer so Scarlett could study each piece in the room. Since it was incredibly old, much of the pottery in the exhibit was barely more than shards. For each one, Luke asked if it was exactly as it should be, and each time Scarlett assured him that it was.

Luke lingered next to a broken piece from a Mesopotamian terra-cotta relief made around 1765 BC, leaning to shine the light under and around it. "This is a really neat piece."

Scarlett shifted into curator mode. "The complete relief that piece comes from was probably strikingly colorful, but time and trials have worn away the paint."

"Fascinating," Luke said. "I'd heard that some of the ancient sculptures we see all the time looked really different in their prime." He grinned at her. "It's nice to have it confirmed by an expert."

"The color would have made a difference, but I think these pieces still carry so much personality. This is actually one of my favorites." The woman sculpted into the shard faced directly out, with a serene expression that was almost a smile. One ear still bore a large earring, though the other side of the shard ended in a jagged break where the earring would have been. The woman had some kind of headdress, though the wear made it hard to guess at what it had originally been.

"I think she was someone who got things done," Luke said.

Scarlett agreed. "She bears a resemblance to the goddess figure in the Burney Relief, also known as the Queen of the Night."

Luke laughed. "Now you've lost me completely. When this exhibit is open again, you'll have to school me on all of this." He walked to the plinth that had helped hide Tasha's body. "This lady is unusual."

The Central American ceramic figure on the plinth couldn't have been more different from the elegant face on the pottery shard. The figure was created from square shapes and had short outstretched arms. Her open-mouthed expression of hunger had an ominous air. Luke aimed his flashlight's beam into the dark mouth. "There's something in there. Is that normal?"

Scarlett yelped. "It is *not*. How could something have gotten into the mouth?"

"I'm more interested in what it is," Luke said. "We need to retrieve it."

"Fine, but we have to be careful. This one is on loan from a major Central American museum, and they'll want it back in exactly the same condition as it was loaned."

"Well, I'll bow to your expertise, but we need to retrieve whatever is in there. It could be evidence in this investigation."

"Right. I have some tools in my office." She left him in the exhibit and hurried to retrieve the bag she kept there. She felt it was always important to be able to examine artifacts safely no matter where she was, so she always kept a small tool kit. The archaeologist in her never completely let go of such habits.

When she returned to the exhibit room, she found Luke still peering into the mouth with his flashlight. She had him hold the light while she teased a scrap of cloth from the figure's mouth with a pair of long tweezers. She suspected it took longer than Luke would have preferred, but she couldn't rush the task. It wouldn't take much to damage the delicate figure. In fact, she was surprised someone had managed to cram something inside without chipping the opening in the first place.

Finally she had it free and could tell that it was a rag. She held it up and Luke shone the light on it. The cloth was still partially crumpled, the wrinkles held in place by what could only be blood—and rather a lot of it.

15

Scarlett lay on her sofa with Cleo sprawled on her chest. The cat's purr rumbled through Scarlett. "You wouldn't be so nice to me if you knew what a giant coward I am."

Cleo butted her head against Scarlett's hand that had foolishly stopped petting her.

Scarlett took the gesture as a request for elaboration and resumed scratching the cat's chin as she talked. "I think Luke is leaving. Moving to Virginia. What do you think of that?"

Cleo yawned, showing sharp white teeth and a curled tongue.

"Don't yawn at me. It's not dull. It's horrible. You're not being very sympathetic."

Cleo closed her eyes and purred louder, proof once more that cats must always have the last word.

Scarlett rubbed Cleo's ears. "You're probably right. I am being dull. It's not as if I don't understand why telling me isn't Luke's top priority." She thought of that horrible cloth they'd found. Since the artifact had not had a rag crammed in its mouth when she'd set it on the plinth, the cloth had to be connected to the murder, but what information might come from it?

At Luke's request, Scarlett had carried the pottery figure itself downstairs to the workrooms and x-rayed it, making sure the murder weapon wasn't somehow lodged inside as well. But the cavity was empty.

"I can't believe you have that machine here," Luke had said.

"We have everything. It's one of the reasons I was so quick to jump at the chance to be curator here. Devon Reed spared no expense when he outfitted all the workrooms. Anything I need to do, I have the equipment to do it."

"Including analyze blood?"

"I could, but wouldn't that compromise evidence?"

"It would, and I'm not asking you to do it," he had said. "I'm simply interested in whether you could." He mused over the cloth, safe inside a plastic bag. "We'll have to call the police so they can go over the special exhibit room again. If they missed this cloth—probably from fear of damaging something priceless—they could have missed other things."

That was why Scarlett was sprawled on her sofa with a cat while her living room slowly drained of daylight. She'd been at the museum for hours while the police processed the scene again and the chief scolded Luke for removing the ceramic figure from the exhibit.

"I knew you'd want to know that it was empty," Luke had replied mildly. "And Scarlett couldn't have something that valuable and delicate leaving the museum. The piece is on loan from another museum that is trusting her to see to its safety. This was the best solution for all concerned."

The chief grumbled but he'd left the artifact with Scarlett, and she appreciated that more than she could say. She'd miss Luke sticking up for her to the chief—another thing to add to her long list of what she'd miss when he left.

Cleo woke with a start when Scarlett's ringtone cut through the quiet. Scarlett snagged her phone from the coffee table where she'd left it in case Luke called her and swiped to answer it without checking the screen. "Any news on the bloodstain?"

"Bloodstain?" her mother, Elaine McCormick, yelped. "Scarlett, what are you up to now?"

Scarlett cringed. "Hi, Mom. How are you?"

"How am I?" Elaine echoed. "How do you think I am? I'm in a panic over my daughter casually discussing things like bloodstains. What are you talking about? Were you injured?"

"No, Mom, I'm fine," Scarlett said. "It's a police thing."

"A police thing involving you? Again? Why am I not surprised?" Elaine chuckled. "You have far more interactions with the police than anyone else I know. I seriously doubt your sister even knows the names of the police officers in Eugene."

"I don't know," Scarlett said. "Vivienne could surprise you. She's a librarian. They know everyone."

"You know what I mean."

"Mom, I'm dating an FBI agent. I'm going to get involved with more police matters than Vivienne." Luke wasn't the source of most of her police contacts, but she hated to give her mother reason to worry. Elaine was an artist, and she should be free to pursue her creative endeavors, not have to fret over her adult daughter on the other side of the country.

"Your cousin Jean is married to a policeman," her mother said. "And I doubt she has seen a single dead body."

"Fine, my life is weird. But to be fair, I signed up for lots of dead bodies when I became an archaeologist like Dad. I just thought they'd be dead longer before I saw them. Did you call for anything in particular?"

"Not really. It's almost Christmas, and I wanted to hear your voice. Please tell me you have some plan for the holiday that doesn't involve dead bodies."

"My plans rarely do," Scarlett said.

"Then how do you keep ending up with them?"

Scarlett sighed. "I don't know. We had a problem at the donor party. I told you about that, right?"

"You told me you intended to have a party to thank the museum's major donors, which I thought was a wonderful idea. Did you take people up in that clock tower you have? Is that how someone died?" Elaine guessed. "Not everyone can manage those spiral stairs, especially in formal wear."

"No, I did not take guests to the clock tower. No one would have enjoyed the view up there at night in winter. California has nothing on your winters in New York, but it's still chilly."

"Then what happened?"

"One of the guests died in my new exhibit."

"The exhibit about ancient women? I'm so sorry, dear. That's terrible. You worked so hard on putting that together. How did the person die?"

"She was murdered," Scarlett said glumly. "I'm sure the police will deal with it. They're very competent. But it is very sad."

"Oh no," her mother murmured in the tone that had always soothed Scarlett's heart. "You weren't nearby when it happened, were you?"

"It happened while we were in the room. Someone shut off the lights, and the woman was killed then."

Elaine sucked air through her teeth in a sympathetic hiss. "Was Luke there?"

"He was."

"Well, thank heavens for that. I hope he's keeping you out of the investigation as much as possible."

"I'm not putting myself in danger, but they do need my help with some things," Scarlett assured her mother, and she felt confident that was the truth at least. She couldn't see how anything she'd done could be putting her in any danger. "Luke is usually with me for my involvement."

"I'm glad to hear that. He has a good head on his shoulders."

"He does."

"I like him, Scarlett. Oh, speaking of good men, could I get your input on your father's Christmas gift? I ordered a really lovely Aran sweater for him, a nod to the fact that we're going to Ireland next year, but I don't think it's going to arrive in time. Now I don't have a gift."

Scarlett's parents traveled a lot, and often came home with all sorts of mementos of their trips, but as far as she knew, it was the first time her mother had considered buying the memento ahead of time. "You're going to Ireland, but you bought an Irish sweater now? Wouldn't it make more sense to buy one when you're in Ireland?"

"I thought it would be a fun reminder that we have that on the agenda," her mother said. "Anyway, forget the sweater. What do I get your father at the last minute that he'll actually use or enjoy?"

Scarlett's father was a retired archaeology professor from Cornell, but Scarlett knew a part of him would always miss the experience of being in the field. Scarlett could relate, and she suspected it was part of what made him so eager to travel during his retirement. "Actually I have one suggestion," she said. "There's a book coming out by an author Dad admires, an anthropologist who specializes in ancient civilization and what their artifacts say about their culture. You should get him that."

"That does sound good. Let me get paper and a pen so I can write this down."

Scarlett waited for her to do so, then rattled off the author's name and the title. "And I expect you'd get extra points if you could find an autographed copy."

"I'm on the hunt," Elaine said grandly.

"Let me know if you need any help with it," Scarlett said, unable to stop a grin.

"I will. Stay safe, dear. I love you."

"I love you too, Mom."

Elaine ended the call, undoubtedly to put some time into searching online for a copy of the book.

Scarlett smiled at the phone in her hand. She had enjoyed the excitement in her mother's voice when she'd suggested the book. Her parents had the perfect marriage as far as Scarlett was concerned. They each had their own interests, but they supported one another in those things. Her mother didn't really have her father's wanderlust, but she loved being with him and she enjoyed painting in the new places where they went. And her father was her mother's biggest fan when it came to her art.

Scarlett had always thought that was the kind of relationship she wanted, one built on both respect and fondness. And she'd begun to think she had that with Luke. That might be why she leaned on him so much—probably too much considering he'd soon be moving away. Long-distance relationships fizzled out eventually, so she knew the best thing would be for them to simply end things when he took the job.

The thought made her eyes fill with tears. "Now, none of that," she scolded herself aloud. "I am a strong, independent woman."

Cleo opened her eyes at the sound of Scarlett's voice. They locked eyes, and Scarlett whispered, "I'm going to miss him so much."

Cleo rubbed her head against Scarlett's hand in sympathy.

Her phone rang again. Luke.

"How are you doing?" Luke asked. "I'm sure finding a bloodstained cloth and then having the police go back through that room was stressful."

"I'd rather no one used a priceless artifact as a hiding place for something so grisly, but if it helps find the murderer, then I'm glad we found it. I really appreciate what you did to prevent the police from seizing that artifact. I don't know how I would have explained that to the museum that owns it."

"All the chief wants is the truth and clean evidence," Luke said.

"There are really only two possible reasons for that cloth. Either it was used to wrap the murder weapon for disposal, which we eliminated by x-raying the artifact, or it was used to wipe the murder weapon so the killer could carry it out."

"But everyone was searched by the police," Scarlett said.

"Right, and no one had any kind of blade. But perhaps it was smuggled out of the exhibit room and hidden somewhere else."

"Those options are limited," Scarlett said. "Everyone was kept on the second-floor landing. We know they didn't carry the weapon downstairs because they were searched on the second floor before they were allowed to leave."

"Which pretty much leaves that landing or your office, if the murderer was one of the people the chief interviewed."

"Unless it was Libby," Scarlett said. "She was all over the second floor. And she had knives. It was the whole explanation for that blood on her clothes and shoe."

"The chief confiscated her knives, but you're right—she would surely have gotten rid of the one she used if she's the killer. I think the entire second floor should be searched. I'll call the chief and suggest it."

Scarlett groaned. "So we won't be opening tomorrow after all."

"Maybe not. I'm sorry."

Scarlett fought down the urge to sigh again. "Do you know if any of Libby's knives tested positive for blood?"

"Haven't heard," he said. "We'll probably hear from the lab on that around the same time that we find out about what was in that coffee urn. The optimistic time frame I was given was tomorrow."

Scarlett's thoughts settled into gloom. "I'm starting to get a phobia of holidays," she said. "This is the second Christmas with a body."

"I'm sure it's not the beginning of a trend," Luke said. "But since you brought up Christmas, when are you putting up your tree?"

"I have a cat," Scarlett said. "And picking up ornaments isn't my favorite pastime. But I love the Christmas tree on the museum landing. I do love all the light and sparkle of Christmas. My lack of a tree is not a symptom of any Scrooge tendencies."

"I never said it was." He paused, then asked, "Are you all right?"

"I'll be fine," Scarlett said. "Life always finds a balance. There are bad things, but there are also amazing and wonderful things." She wasn't sure how the holiday could possibly balance out, considering it contained both a murder and Luke moving away, but she still believed something positive would be on the way.

"That's a good attitude," Luke said. "Say, do you want me to come over? I could pick up some takeout."

Scarlett froze, suddenly chilled to the bone. *This is it. This is when he plans to tell me about the promotion.* She wanted him to tell her, so she could begin to process the change that was coming. But suddenly she wasn't ready. If she could put off that awful conversation, she was desperate to do so.

"It's always great to see you," she said. "But I think I'm going to veg out with a book and a cat."

"That sounds nice," he said, but his tone was disappointed. "Scarlett, are you sure you're okay?"

"Of course. I'm resilient," she assured him, pleased to hear her voice sounded normal enough, despite the tears stinging her eyes.

"I'm sure I'll see you tomorrow. If you change your mind, call me. I'll be right over."

After they finished the call, Scarlett eased Cleo off her and stood, stretching. "Coward," she whispered to herself on the way to the kitchen. She made a sandwich, slicing the bread from a homemade loaf Greta had given her a couple days prior.

Scarlett remembered Greta's warning that she wasn't exactly a master baker yet. "Everyone seems to be learning to make bread," Greta had said. "I thought I was missing out on something, so I'm giving it a try."

The bread was good, but when Scarlett finished piling her sandwich with crisp lettuce, slices of turkey and some sharp cheese, she realized she wasn't hungry at all. "Maybe later," she said, wrapping up the food and setting it aside.

She'd barely stowed the plastic wrap in the drawer when she heard a car door slam outside. It sounded as if the car was right in front of the house. Someone must have pulled up beside her car in order for the noise to be that clear.

I must have left Luke more worried than I thought.

She stood in the kitchen, waiting for the sound of someone on the front step and a knock at the door, but none came. That was odd. Scarlett headed outside and saw her car was alone in the driveway. She also saw the interior light was on in her car, suggesting the door had been open recently.

As Scarlett trotted to the car, she tried to recall if she'd engaged the lock. Before opening the door, she peered up and down the street, but saw no other cars. She lifted the handle as delicately as possible, hoping to not smudge fingerprints. If someone had stolen something from her car, she'd end up talking to the police for the second time that day.

She expected the interior to be a mess, strewn with the contents of the glove box, but everything was perfectly normal—except for a note taped to the steering wheel. The note was half a page of printer paper and had three words, printed in a large block font.

She deserved it!

16

On Monday morning, Scarlett felt a whirl of emotions as she walked into the Reed Museum, carrying a bottle of cleaner for the coffee-stained marble upstairs. She paused just inside the doors to take in the glittering Christmas decorations in the expansive foyer. She still loved the beautiful white-and-silver decorations and the festive air, but it was hard not to feel the holiday decor wasn't quite appropriate after the weekend's events.

And I claimed not to be a Scrooge. She knew part of her mood had been brought on by the note she'd found in her car.

She hadn't called the police or even told Luke about the note. She wasn't sure how seriously the police would take the incident since nothing had been stolen. She couldn't even be certain she'd locked the car. She'd been so preoccupied. Luke would have taken the note seriously, but she didn't want to worry him, not when there was nothing he could really do. Ultimately, she'd decided to decide later.

She strode across the lobby, going over the tasks she'd need to accomplish before the museum opened. A tall cup of coffee was at the top of her list, but talking to Winnie came a close second, as soon as she finished cleaning up the coffee stain. She'd need to discuss a plan for keeping guests away from the new exhibit while it remained a crime scene.

Allie and Greta stood at the counter of Burial Grounds. Greta wore a bright Christmas-themed pin. She seemed to have an almost endless supply of them. The current one featured a gold-colored Christmas tree with brightly colored rhinestone ornaments.

"Hello, Scarlett," Greta said. "How are you?"

"Stressed but functional," Scarlett answered honestly. "And in desperate need of coffee."

Greta pointed at the bottle of floor cleaner. "You taking over for the cleaning staff?"

"It's for a coffee stain upstairs," Scarlett said. "The urn was turned over. I mopped up the mess, but it left a mark."

"Right," Greta said. "I scrubbed that up already."

"The museum has some impressive cleaners," Allie added. "You didn't have to bring your own."

Scarlett looked at the bottle in her hand. "I don't know where my head was." She set the bottle of cleaner on the counter. "Can I leave this down here and get it later? I need coffee and then a chat with Winnie."

"No problem," Allie said. "And I'll give you coffee and a surprise."

Scarlett groaned. "I'm not at all sure I'm up for any surprises."

"You'll be up for this one. Hold on for coffee first."

"Please," Scarlett said.

When Allie handed over a tall cup of coffee, she also offered a piece of paper.

"What's this?" Scarlett asked before taking a sip of the brew.

"A sketch of the special exhibit room," Allie said. She tapped the different-colored dots on the page. "I've marked where everyone was when the lights went out." She pointed to the edge of the paper. "Here's the legend for the dots that explains who each dot represents."

"This is a fantastic idea." Scarlett studied the paper. "How did you know where everyone was?"

"I know where you and Luke were, because everyone was looking at you," Allie explained. "And I assume poor Mrs. Portland was near where her body ended up so I marked her there. Plus, I knew where

I was. I was standing near Maya Shepherd, so I marked her down. Those were the ones I knew from memory."

Greta spoke up then. "I showed Allie where Hal and I were standing. But I wasn't sure where Angelique and her husband were. We thought maybe you'd remember since you were facing everyone."

"I was," Scarlett agreed. "I wish I'd paid more attention. I was so wrapped up in my speech." She closed her eyes and tried to remember, picturing the room and the artifacts since she knew them so well, then imagining the people in the places the map had shown her. But where were Angelique and Rupert?

Her eyes popped open. "I remember. They weren't standing together. There was tension between them outside so they weren't standing together in the room, but I know they were together in the dark because I heard them, so one or the other must have moved." She tapped on the map. "I'm fairly sure Rupert was there, but I honestly don't remember where Angelique was." She stared harder at the map as if she could make the information appear, but ultimately shook her head.

Allie tugged the paper from Scarlett's hand. "I'll mark Rupert. Then we'll need to find someone who remembers Angelique's position."

"I'll ask Luke," Scarlett said. "He may have noticed."

Allie snorted at that. "Luke had eyes for nothing and no one but you. I remember that well enough. The man is the definition of moral support."

"He is that." Scarlett realized the remark sounded almost sad, and hoped neither of her friends would comment on it. Thankfully they were both absorbed in the map as Allie made a dot for Rupert.

Scarlett wouldn't mind talking to Allie about Luke's promotion, but she felt disloyal at the thought. It was Luke's news to tell, not hers. Plus she wasn't exactly eager to admit to some light snooping, not even to Allie. She needed to give Luke time to tell her.

"I had a thought," Greta said. "I could ask Hal where Angelique was standing. He notices everything. It's part of his theater training, where they have to memorize who goes where on the set."

"Once we ask Hal about Angelique, one of us will bring the map up to your office," Allie suggested. "Possibly me. With more coffee."

"That would be great. Thanks. Have either of you seen Winnie? I'd rather not wander all over the museum to find her."

"She grabbed a coffee on her way downstairs to the security office," Allie said. "I haven't seen her since."

"I'll check there first." Scarlett raised her coffee cup. "Thanks for the best coffee in Crescent Harbor."

Allie grinned. "I live to please."

"Speaking of Winnie," Greta said. "She mentioned that the police were here again yesterday and searched the whole second floor. Does that mean that floor is closed today? I'll need to tell all the docents."

"No, thankfully. They finished the search. Only the special exhibit is still closed."

"That's good," Allie said. "The place will be packed today. Folks in this town love a mystery."

"How would they even know about it?" Scarlett asked. "I checked the paper, and the murder wasn't in it yet."

"Gossip moves in mysterious ways," Greta said. "But I'd be ready for media people asking questions today."

Scarlett agreed. "I'll have my 'no comment' ready."

She left her friends and headed to the basement.

When she reached the security office, Scarlett found Winnie watching video from Saturday night. "Just what I came to ask you about," Scarlett said. "Have you found anything interesting?"

"I believe so," Winnie said. "Come and see this." She replayed the recording of the side door of the museum, then froze it at the point where Val appeared. "We caught Myers's entrance."

She started the video again and Scarlett watched Val open the door and let Myers in. Myers amiably pounded the young man on the back, but Val frowned and spoke urgently to the other man. Myers waved him off and walked away out of range of the camera with Val following.

"There's a time stamp," Winnie pointed it out. "I've compared it to the time stamp on the camera that recorded the arrival of the caterer and Val. It appears that letting Myers in was one of the first things Val did."

"How did he open the door without the alarm going off?" Scarlett asked.

Winnie pointed again. "See those wooden crates right there? That stuff belonged to the caterer. She used this door to come in and out, so we had to disengage that alarm. I should have put a guard on it. That's on me."

"You couldn't have known." Scarlett frowned at the screen. "So where did Myers hang out all that time between when Val let him in and when he actually crashed the party?"

"I have that information too." Winnie switched to another camera that showed Myers slipping behind the huge chair where Santa had sat during the Children's Holiday Cheer event earlier in the day. The chair and the Christmas tree beside him hid the man perfectly. "This particular video doesn't show Myers again until around the time the guests arrived. We don't have a camera that shows exactly where he was."

"Possibly hiding so he could watch for Tasha?" Scarlett suggested.

"Maybe," Winnie agreed. "We've added some cameras so not all of them focus on exhibits, but it's still easy enough to avoid them if your goal isn't to sneak in and steal things."

"We know he eventually came upstairs." Scarlett said. "Do you have video of him leaving after that?"

"No," Winnie said. "We caught him briefly on one camera as he headed across the first floor, but nothing from that actual door to outside."

"Why is that?" Scarlett asked.

"Because of this," Winnie switched to the camera view of Val letting Myers in the door. She sped the camera up and the feed focused on the door for some time, then suddenly shifted radically until it pointed directly at the floor.

"What happened?" Scarlett asked.

"Someone hit the camera with something," Winnie said. "The camera is mounted too high to reach by hand, so someone must have thrown something. In order to ensure it would move the camera's angle so radically, it had to be something fairly heavy. Plus, I've examined the camera itself and there's a crack in the housing. I'm thinking someone threw a rock. I have some of my people searching the museum inside and out to try to find a rock or something equally heavy in a place where it shouldn't be, but that won't work if the person retrieved their projectile and took it with them."

"That sounds challenging," Scarlett said. "The time stamp on that shift is considerably after Val let Myers in. In fact, it may even be after the guests started to arrive. I wasn't watching the clock, but that sounds about right. Is it after Myers moved from his hiding place?"

"It is," Winnie said. "But if he left his hiding place and headed to the door to damage that camera, he must have known exactly where the cameras were and purposefully avoided them when he didn't want us to be able to track his movements."

"Or someone else knocked the camera out of alignment and we don't see Myers heading that way because he didn't go there," Scarlett said.

"Anything is possible," Winnie said, but her tone suggested she didn't consider it probable."

Scarlett frowned at the screen. They knew what they'd already known—that Val had let Myers in. But whether Myers left when he said couldn't be confirmed. "Have you checked to see if Myers could have left by another door?"

"I don't know how he would have," Winnie said. "But I'm still going through all the available footage. It's a lot. We have so many cameras, and even with a fairly narrow window of opportunity, it's still a lot to check, especially since some of the time Myers is barely a flash in the corner of the few camera angles we've already found him on."

"I appreciate all your work," Scarlett said.

"Once I finish going through all of this, I'll call the police and offer to pass on copies of the footage. With any luck, we'll have a rock for them as well."

"Good work. By the way, do you have a plan for putting someone outside the special exhibit? While the museum is open, I need someone in a security uniform there at all times. I'm not convinced crime scene tape alone will keep out the truly curious."

"I have someone up there right now," Winnie said. "And a roster of folks to take short shifts. I want to change them out often enough to keep them alert."

"Thanks. You're the best. Let me know if you find anything new."

"I will," Winnie assured her.

As she left the security office, Scarlett pondered what the damaged camera proved. Well, for one, it meant Myers could have been in the museum during the murder, since they had no proof that he'd left when he'd claimed. He'd been out of his hiding spot in time to have wrecked the camera, but how could he have gotten into the special exhibit?

Scarlett rode up in the elevator, thinking about the exhibit rooms. Because of fire codes, every room in the museum had more than one exit. That meant no one would be trapped in a room if the door they'd used to enter was blocked. For all of the large, permanent exhibits as well as the special exhibits on the first floor, visitor traffic was funneled through each room, using both doors. But the special exhibits on the second floor were different. The rooms were smaller, and guests entered and exited through the same door. There were emergency doors, but they weren't used regularly. The single entry and exit point gave the special exhibits a feeling of exclusivity.

Scarlett stepped out of the elevator and headed for the stairs to the second floor at a trot, picturing the inside of the special exhibit room that housed *The Forgotten Women* exhibit. It had an entrance that opened onto the large second floor landing. That was the one door anyone could easily see from inside, but another door, painted all black, opened to a cramped utility hallway at the rear of the room. That door and the utility closet were used so rarely Scarlett had forgotten they existed.

Entry to that utility hall was through another door, not far from the second set of restrooms. The hall door was narrow and marked *Staff Only*, which suggested it might be a storage closet. No one would assume it would allow them access to the special exhibit.

As Scarlett stood on the second-floor landing, staring at the crime scene tape and the guard standing nearby, she remembered the sight of Libby in the restroom. She'd sensed the woman was lying about her reason for sneaking away, but she'd ultimately assumed Libby was there to attempt to wash away the bloodstain on her sleeve. Could she really have been there because of its closeness to another access point to the crime scene? Could she have used it to retrieve the murder weapon and dispose of it, for instance?

Could Libby be a killer?

17

The utility hallway to the exhibit was not considered part of the crime scene since none of the guests would have known about it, so Scarlett headed that way. There were no cameras in the narrow hall since it never contained exhibits and was rarely used at all. Scarlett preferred using the large main doors to the special exhibits, even when loading in artifacts. It was easier.

As Scarlett stepped into the utility hall, she was reminded of another reason she didn't use it. The hall was weakly lit and the walls were painted black. The dimness and the narrow confines of the hall made the space uncomfortable.

Scarlett walked the length of the hall several times, paying special attention to the corners and the floor to be certain nothing had been dropped. As soon as she felt certain she hadn't missed anything, she moved to the rear door of the special exhibit room and opened it. The door was tight in the frame to help it blend in with the wall. As a result, it made a dragging sound as it opened. She'd forgotten about it, since she hadn't opened the door in some time. The sound wasn't loud, but it was certainly audible. Had she heard it on the night of the murder? She tried to remember, but she wasn't sure. She was confident she would have heard something.

Feeling none the wiser, she gave up and left. She was all too happy to exit the creepy hall and stood a while in the wider expanse beyond, soaking up the light and breathing deeply.

Once she felt less jumpy, she headed for the restroom. The room had been searched, so Scarlett wasn't sure what she thought she would find that the police had missed, but she knew she wouldn't be able to relax until she'd checked. She scanned the room, trying to think like a desperate killer with a murder weapon to hide. The restroom was far smaller than the other ladies' room on the second floor and lacked the chaise seating. It also lacked any obvious place to hide a murder weapon.

Scarlett knelt so she could peer under the counters. She didn't find anything. "What did you expect to find?"

She couldn't answer her own question, but she was sure she was missing something. Maybe something she'd seen. She moved until she stood with her back to the door and scanned the room again. It was where they'd found Libby after she'd left police interrogation without being dismissed.

Scarlett tried to re-create the image in her mind. The caterer had been sitting on the counter when Scarlett had entered, but that didn't mean she'd been there the whole time. In the quiet of the museum, she might have heard Luke and Scarlett coming. They hadn't been particularly stealthy. So maybe she'd gone as far from where she'd put the knife as possible.

Scarlett thought of the dampness on Libby's sleeve. What if that had come as much from disposing of a knife as from trying to get rid of blood? Scarlett wondered if she should stick her hand into the plumbing to search for the knife, but she quickly came up with all sorts of reasons why she should leave the task to the police. For all she knew, someone had already checked.

The ringtone on her phone had never been more welcome since it gave Scarlett one more reason why she shouldn't get any closer to the plumbing. She answered, and the police chief's deep voice rumbled into her ear. "I need you to come down to the station and give a statement today. I'm told you weren't on my list of appointments."

"I'll come right away," Scarlett said. "Tell me, have you heard from Winnie yet?"

"I have," he said. "I've sent an officer to check out the evidence Winnie found."

"Couldn't she have emailed the video footage?"

"Probably," the chief said. "But she couldn't have emailed the rock."

"She found the rock?" Scarlett pulled the phone away from her face and checked her text messages. Sure enough, Winnie had reported that one of her people had found a smooth rock shoved into one of the planters and she was going to give it to the police.

The chief responded while Scarlett was scanning Winnie's text. "One of her people did. We don't know that it's the object used to damage the camera, but she is certain it wasn't normally in the planter where it was found."

"She's right," Scarlett said. "We don't keep rocks in the planters. Too tempting for kids."

"Is there anything else my officer should check?" the chief asked.

"Did anyone check the plumbing in the rear restrooms on the second floor?" Scarlett asked.

"Not as far as I know," the chief said. "Why?"

"I realized someone could have entered and exited the special exhibit through the rear door. The utility hall behind the two special exhibit rooms on this floor is narrow, and the door is small, intended to suggest that it's a supply closet. With the inner doors painted black, I honestly forget there is a second door, but it's a requirement in case of fire." She realized she was babbling and stopped.

"I'm aware of the door and the hallway," the chief said. "One of my officers went through the door last night when searching the crime scene. He found no sign that anyone had been through it before."

"Yes, but what if it's how someone got into the exhibit to commit the murder, someone like Libby Proctor? That restroom where we found her is near the utility hallway. So if she hid the knife near that door and then returned to get it and dispose of it, she could have dropped it in the plumbing when she was in this restroom. Her sleeve was wet."

"I thought the sleeve was wet because she'd tried to wash away blood," the chief said.

"Maybe it's both."

"I'll have the officer check." Then the chief's voice grew amused. "I'm surprised you haven't pulled the pipes apart yourself."

"I thought that was a job for the police," Scarlett said.

"That's never stopped you before," Rodriguez pointed out.

Scarlett couldn't argue with that.

The Crescent Harbor Police department was located in city hall, taking up a relatively small space considering the department did more community service than crime solving. Crescent Harbor was a fairly quiet tourist town, and the police had bike patrols, rescue teams, beach patrol, and a school liaison officer. Still, Scarlett had learned that the department was more than capable. Luke respected both their competence and their dedication, and that went a long way in Scarlett's book. She'd also worked with them several times and been impressed with their competence.

She pushed through the glass doors leading into the department and immediately attracted the attention of receptionist Raven Flowers. A string of gold garland and a cheery snowman added a dash of festive cheer to the front of the reception desk. Scarlett suspected that was

Raven's doing. The receptionist often did her best to lighten the mood whenever she felt everyone was getting worn down, which included bringing in baked goods to share with her coworkers.

Raven was in her early thirties and had pretty green eyes and sleek black hair that hung to her shoulders. She had the kind of smile that disarmed people, making her a real asset on the reception desk.

"Hi, Scarlett," Raven said. "The chief is expecting you."

"Thanks. Have you seen Luke today?"

Raven shook her head. "I know the chief has spoken to him."

Scarlett took a deep breath and squared her shoulders. She was glad she'd gone for a power suit when she'd dressed that morning. It made her feel more confident, even if nothing else about the day did. "Okay, I'm ready."

"Good luck," Raven said. "And when you come out, stop here. I made snickerdoodles, and I kept one for you."

"You are a gem," Scarlett said.

After Raven buzzed her through the door, she made her way to the chief's desk, ready to give her account of the party and everything else that had popped up since.

The chief greeted her cordially, if not as warmly as Raven had.

"Thank you for coming down," he said as he led her into a private room for their conversation. "I have spoken to Luke, so I have probably already heard everything you have to say, but it's good to have a clear record from everyone. You should be aware that I will be recording our conversation."

"I understand. That's not a problem. Do you have any strong suspects?"

Rodriguez grunted. "I do, but let's focus on what you have for me."

"Well, I do have something Luke didn't tell you." She reached into her bag and pulled out the note she'd found in her car and handed it over to the chief. It was encased in a nice new kitchen storage bag.

She doubted it was covered in any kind of valuable evidence, but she didn't want to discard that possibility completely.

The chief studied the note. "And where did you find this?"

"In my car," Scarlett said. "Last night I was making something to eat, and I heard the sound of a car door closing from right outside. I thought someone was coming to visit, but I now believe it was my car door closing. When no one came to the door, I went outside, saw my interior light was still on and found this taped to the steering wheel."

"Did you lock your car?"

Scarlett winced. "Maybe not. I usually do, but I'll admit I've been distracted in light of the murder. I examined the lock this morning and didn't see any fresh scratches."

"Is your car here?" the chief asked.

Scarlett confirmed that it was, and the chief asked for her keys and then called for someone to go out and look it over.

"And this note is the only odd communication you've had?" the chief asked.

Scarlett winced. "Not exactly. I got a phone call on the night of the donor party. It came in before I left the house. Anyway, I answered the call and someone said they were sorry and that 'it' was necessary. I don't know for certain that the call has anything to do with the murder. It could have been a prank."

"Was the caller a man or a woman?" the chief asked.

"I couldn't tell. The person was whispering. I could barely make out what they said."

"It sounds to me that both communications are about justifying the murder," the chief said. "And since they're directed at you, it suggests familiarity with you. Why would the person want you specifically to feel their actions were justified?"

Scarlett hadn't considered that. She did know all of the guests at the party—not well, but she'd had positive encounters with all of them before the party. "Well," Scarlett said. "I represent the museum, so if the person felt guilty about involving the museum, that could be the reason."

"Possibly. How well do you know Myers Portland?"

"I'd talked to him a few times," Scarlett said. "Before the divorce and always along with Tasha. He was polite, if a bit full of himself. The contact I've had with him since reflects a different man, a broken one."

The chief frowned but didn't comment on her assessment. "Could the voice on the phone have been Myers Portland?"

"I suppose, but it could have been anyone." Scarlett risked a question. "Have you checked into Libby Proctor and whether she has any connection to Tasha? The utility hallway access to the special exhibits could have been her way in. She could have gone in before we did and left when Luke opened the door. Every eye was on the light pouring in through the main door. No one would have noticed the door opening into the dark utility hall at the rear of the room."

"That's an interesting theory," the chief said. "But it also works for Myers Portland. He could have reached the second floor and used the same hall to slip into the exhibit, and left the same way."

"That would be a lot harder. There were still people on the landing."

"Granted," the chief said. "But we know he had the help of Val Antonov. And he has a motive—something we haven't found for the caterer."

"Unless she was paid to do it," Scarlett suggested.

The chief actually smiled at that. "You think someone paid the caterer to be a hit man."

Scarlett knew his amusement was probably justified. It did sound ridiculous worded that way, but she still wasn't sure she believed Myers was capable of murdering his ex-wife. "So Myers is your prime suspect?"

"I think I'll keep that to myself," the chief said. "But I will tell you that we don't suspect you or any of the museum staff."

"I'm glad to hear that," Scarlett replied. "I've always had the utmost faith and confidence in my team."

"Now," the chief said, "begin at your arrival at the museum on Saturday night and walk me through the events as you remember them. Don't leave anything out."

Scarlett retrieved a notebook from her purse. "I brought some notes to help me remember."

The chief inclined his head slightly and waited.

Scarlett took a deep breath and launched into her statement.

The chief listened attentively, though she knew he'd heard it all before. He asked for clarification a few times, but mostly remained quiet through to the end.

When she was done, he said, "Thank you. Your testimony agrees with Luke's. You've both been a huge help to the investigation."

"I'm happy to help however I can. You know that. And speaking of Luke, he was going to look into a bad business deal between Rupert Milston and Adrian Belsky, Tasha's father. He wondered if it might have given Rupert a motive."

"He told me," the chief said. "And we're checking it out, but it seems extremely unlikely. If anything comes of it, I'm sure Luke will tell you."

"Probably so," Scarlett agreed, wishing she actually believed that given how much Luke wasn't telling her lately.

A tap came to the interview room door, and the officer came in to hand over Scarlett's keys. "There's no sign that the car was broken into."

"I guess I forgot to lock it," Scarlett said. She wasn't overly surprised, but the warming in her cheeks reflected that she was a little embarrassed.

The chief thanked the officer, then escorted Scarlett out of the room, assuring her that the investigation was progressing and things should return to normal at the museum soon.

"I'll be glad for that," she said.

She was most of the way to her car, nibbling on the snickerdoodle Raven had given her on the way out, when she saw one of the Crescent Harbor police cars pull into a space near the building and unload someone from the back seat. The man they hauled out wore handcuffs and held his head low in a posture of utter defeat. Scarlett recognized him in an instant. Myers Portland. As she watched the officers lead him into the station, she had no further doubt. The chief believed he'd found who killed Tasha: her ex-husband.

18

Back at the museum, Scarlett tried to convince herself that the investigation was over and she didn't need to give it any further thought. She failed. She could never quite put the image of a dejected Myers being led into the station out of her mind. Myers had a motive, and she knew that most murderers were those closest to the victim. He made sense.

Unfortunately Scarlett couldn't quite believe it.

"They didn't simply arrest a convenient person," she reminded herself as she stared at the pile of paperwork she couldn't concentrate on.

Her reasonable tone did nothing to convince her. She understood why the police felt confident, but she disagreed. There were too many people mixed up in the whole affair who were behaving oddly. The malaise stayed with her to the end of the day, and it wasn't helped along by Luke's failure to show up at the museum. Not that they'd made any plans for him to do so. He had a real job too, but she felt slightly adrift, and his presence always grounded her.

At two, her doldrums were briefly lifted when Allie walked in with a tall cup of coffee and the map she'd promised. "Sorry I wasn't up here earlier," Allie said. "The museum has been swamped. I think Hal and Greta are being run off their feet by the crowd."

Scarlett had noticed that when she'd moved through the museum, but the strangeness hadn't sunk in. "I guess murder does bring in the crowds."

"An extreme way to increase business." Allie set the coffee on Scarlett's desk, then the map beside it. "I have a tentative dot for Angelique. Hal thought maybe he'd seen her, but he wasn't sure. I still added it."

Scarlett had forgotten about the map. The police would possibly appreciate it, even if they did think they had the case solved. She would scan the map and email it to the chief. Scarlett stood. "Let me put this in the scanner."

"No problem." Allie leaned against the desk and studied Scarlett. "I know why I'm wiped out, but you're not yourself at all. Was the trip to the police station that bad?"

Scarlett blinked in surprise. "How did you know I was at the police department?"

"Winnie. Don't ask me how she knew. That woman knows everything. Was the questioning that tough? Hot lights and snarled questions?"

Scarlett slid the map into the scanner and pressed *Start*. "Hardly. The questioning wasn't the problem. I saw Myers marched into the station. They've arrested him."

"That surely isn't a shock," Allie said.

"Not a shock, but disappointing. And I'm not convinced it's right." Scarlett groaned. "I know the police know more than I do, but there are still so many loose ends. I guess I want everything wrapped up neatly, but nothing in my life can be so neat."

"Nothing?" Allie leaped on the word with a speed that reminded Scarlett of Cleo pouncing on a bug. "So it's not only the case that has you in a funk. Spill. What's going on?"

"Nothing. Well, something, but nothing I can talk about. I don't even know."

Allie squinted at her. "That was confusing."

"Welcome to my world." Scarlett leaned against her desk beside Allie. She sipped her coffee and wished Luke would come by. "I emailed you a copy of the map."

"Thanks. What are you and Luke doing for Christmas?" Allie asked, as if she'd read Scarlett's mind.

"I'm spending the day with a book and a cat," Scarlett said. "Luke is spending it with his family."

"You two haven't broken up, have you?" Allie asked as her smile dipped to a frown.

"No, of course not," Scarlett said. *Not yet. Not until he leaves for Virginia.*

"Didn't he invite you to come to Christmas?" Allie asked.

"Yes, but it's his family time."

Allie's frown deepened. "Scarlett, I love you like a sister, but sometimes I don't understand you at all."

"Sometimes I feel the same way about myself," Scarlett admitted.

Allie studied her a moment longer, then stood. "I give up trying to make sense of your life. For now, anyway. I need to do some more Christmas shopping, so I have to get going. I have never understood people who shop early. They rob themselves of the best part."

"The crowds?" Scarlett said. "Or the picked-over merchandise?"

"Wow, you're a Scrooge today. I'm out of here before you dampen my Christmas spirit."

"Ho, ho, ho," Scarlett said by way of goodbye. She dropped back into her desk chair, picked up her pen, and then pulled a pile of paperwork toward her. She even got most of it done before she tidied up at five and went home. She made sure to pack the copy of Allie's map that she'd printed in her bag before she left. She had emailed the chief a copy, but hadn't heard from him about it. She supposed he didn't consider it a priority.

It wasn't until Scarlett was settled on the sofa with a cup of tea, the map, and Cleo that she began to recognize how tightly she was wound as the stress slowly eased from her body. Cleo sprawled across her lap, occasionally raising her head to bump it against the map as Scarlett studied it.

To keep the cat from batting at the paper, Scarlett stroked her absently with one hand, but her focus was on the map. She contemplated each person relative to their position near the rear door of the exhibit. If the police were right and Myers was the killer, that meant he must have come and gone through that door. He would have hidden somewhere near the door, but then had to move through the people in the complete darkness to reach Tasha. How could he have done that?

She traced possible routes with her finger, but each time she was stunned by the amount of skill it would have taken not to run into someone. Then she remembered people using the flashlights on their phones, which would have added an extra level of difficulty. Myers would have had to get by everyone, and then he would have had to avoid being caught in the light of the phones. Granted the light hadn't spread far, but it would have added to the risk. Scarlett wasn't at all sure she could have managed to slip through the darkness and reach Tasha, and she knew the exact placement of every exhibit. Myers wouldn't have had that, unless he'd memorized it awfully quickly.

She thought of the ranting man who had disrupted the party before the murder. She'd been fairly sure then that Myers had been drinking, which would have made a stealth-based murder even harder. He could have been pretending to be impaired in order to make himself less of a suspect. But then why would he create a disturbance at all if he were trying to avoid suspicion?

Scarlett felt as if her thoughts were going round and round like a hamster on a wheel, expending energy but not accomplishing anything.

Cleo had fallen asleep, and Scarlett's own eyes felt heavy. She knew she absolutely should not take a nap. She'd be up half the night if she did, but the temptation was difficult to resist. She'd almost succumbed when she heard a knock at the door.

Scarlett eased Cleo off her lap, bringing a grumbling mew from the cat. Then she unfolded her long legs and headed for the door. A twist of fear hit her as she touched the knob. What if the mysterious caller and note writer was on her step, ready to make a more direct contact? Scarlett straightened her shoulders and raised her chin. *In that case, I'll give them a piece of my mind.* She yanked the door open.

Luke stood in her entryway. He held up a bag from Rosita's, one of their favorite restaurants. "I brought dinner. I assumed you haven't eaten because you've been obsessing about the murder."

"I hate being predictable." Scarlett stepped aside to let him in.

"Maybe I'm perceptive," Luke suggested, still smiling. "After all, I am a federal agent."

"Oh, right. I knew you were busy doing something." Even to Scarlett, the joke sounded flat.

He carried the bag to the kitchen counter. While he unloaded the bag, Scarlett collected silverware and plates.

"I have news on the coffee urn, by the way," he said.

"What's that?" Scarlett had forgotten about the bad coffee, another detail that made no sense.

"The lab determined it was denatonium benzoate."

Scarlett took a taco from one of the containers. "I have no idea what that is. Some kind of poison?"

"No. Val was right. He wasn't poisoning anyone. Though that doesn't necessarily mean he won't be facing charges. Not only is food tampering a crime, but he aided and abetted a killer by letting him in and cutting the lights. He was a foolish young man, and there will be an investigation into his actions."

"That's assuming Myers is the killer," Scarlett said.

"The chief believes he is."

Scarlett let that go while she took a bite from her taco. Finally she asked, "So what exactly is that chemical stuff?"

"Denatonium benzoate is used to denature alcohol, but it's also put into dangerous household liquids to keep young children from drinking them. Apparently it's the bitterest chemical in existence."

"Where would you get something like that?" Scarlett asked.

"It's easily available online," Luke said. "I checked and found over a dozen different places to get it."

"So anyone could have bought it."

"Pretty much." Luke bit into his taco while Scarlett considered that.

"Do you agree with the chief?" Scarlett asked. "Are you convinced Myers is the killer?"

Luke put his taco down and shifted on the stool. "He is an excellent suspect. I don't think Myers has been completely honest, and he has motive. From what the chief told me this afternoon, Myers hasn't helped himself much."

"What do you mean?" Scarlett asked.

"He told the chief that he learned the best way to get into the museum from an anonymous note left on his car. That's where the idea of making a grand romantic gesture supposedly came from."

"And you don't believe him?" Scarlett asked.

"It seems far-fetched, especially since Myers says he lost the note. Still, I always have my doubts until definitive evidence is found. Right now, we don't have that. We have a lot of possibilities, but few certainties."

"Do you know if the chief has any explanation for why Myers would want the coffee to taste bad?" Scarlett asked. "It makes absolutely no sense."

"I've noticed that," Luke said. "The chief doesn't have any more answers to it than we do, but I'm sure the pieces will fit eventually."

"I wish we had been able to get the note Val says he got and the one Myers described," Scarlett said. "Then they could be compared to the note I got."

"The note you got?"

"The chief didn't tell you?"

"No, he didn't."

Scarlett explained about the slamming door and the note in her car. "I gave it to the chief when he took my statement this morning."

"I'm not happy that you went outside alone to investigate," Luke said. "And it worries me that you're potentially getting notes from a killer."

"Or maybe it's from someone who simply agrees with what the killer did," Scarlett suggested. "We know Tasha didn't have a large fan club."

"Either way, why didn't you call me?"

Because I need to get used to doing things without you. Scarlett bit back the words and said, "I'm telling you now. Luke, I'm not a damsel in distress. I've lived alone for years. I'm not going to start being afraid to walk out my door."

"I get that, but I worry."

"I'm sorry," Scarlett said. "I didn't mean to make you worry."

Luke didn't comment further on the note. He hopped up and began clearing their plates. "I think there's no time like the present to get a few more answers. Let's go over to Val's apartment and see if he's remembered anything now that he's had some time to think about it."

Scarlett could tell there were unspoken feelings behind the brisk cleaning, but she didn't question it. She ate the last bite of her taco and helped straighten up the kitchen. She could be completely professional if that would get her through however many days it was going to take Luke to admit he was leaving her.

The drive to Val's apartment in Luke's car was fairly quiet. Luke commented once or twice on Christmas decorations and lights they passed, and Scarlett said something positive each time he did, but the tension between them was palpable. For Scarlett, the weight of things unsaid pressed against her chest. She was nearly ready to confess to snooping in his car simply to get the topic out so they could talk about it, but before she could get up the nerve, they were at Val's apartment building.

Luke practically launched from the car, rushing around to get Scarlett's door.

"I can open my own door," Scarlett muttered as she unbuckled, but she thanked him when the door swung open.

They heard shouting from inside the apartment even before they reached it. Were the people who'd searched the apartment inside? Luke pounded on the door, and Val opened it. He was red-faced but didn't show any sign of fright. A woman stood behind Val. She was a few years older, but had strikingly similar features.

"Miss Antonov?" Luke said. "How do you do? I'm Luke Anderson, and this is Scarlett McCormick. You were working when we were here Saturday night."

"How do you do?" Val's sister was visibly upset, even frightened.

"May we come in?" Luke asked. "We want to talk to you. Unofficially."

"I guess," Val said sullenly. He stepped away to let them in, but his expression didn't lighten. "But only for a minute. I'm really busy."

Once they were inside, Scarlett shut the door behind them and Luke launched right in. "Miss Antonov, I'm a federal agent. I don't know if your brother told you about us."

Val's sister nodded as she widened her eyes. "He's told me some."

"Good," Luke said cheerfully as if everything in the apartment were completely normal. "I'm not officially working this case, but I thought you still could talk to me about denatonium benzoate."

Though Val's expression didn't change, his sister's eyes bulged. "It's not my fault. I didn't know what Val wanted to do with the stuff. It's not my fault."

"Stop talking!" Val snapped, but the damage was already done.

Luke smiled at Val. "We need to chat about exactly what role you played in Tasha Portland's murder. And this time, I recommend you tell me the truth."

19

"I had nothing to do with the murder," Val insisted. "Nothing. This is not what you think."

"Then you'd better tell us what we should be thinking," Luke said. "And maybe we should all sit down while we do it."

"Sure," Val's sister said, ignoring her brother's scowls and waving a hand toward the sofa. "Please come and sit. Do you want some coffee?" Then she must have remembered they were there because of something Val had put into coffee, because she winced. "Or tea?"

"No, thank you." Scarlett noticed the apartment was quite different from their previous visit. It had been cleaned and tidied. She spotted careful stitching on one of the previously slashed sofa cushions as she sat. "No need to go to that trouble. I don't think I heard your first name?"

"Nia," the woman said, twisting her hands. "I'm Nia Antonov."

Scarlett settled on the sofa, careful to avoid the torn cushion. Luke sat beside her, but he stayed quiet, apparently happy to let her try to make a connection with the distressed woman. "And you work nights?"

"Yes. I'm a chemist."

"Is that how you had access to the chemical Val used?" Scarlett asked.

Nia frowned at her brother, who was leaning against the wall with his arms crossed. "Yes. We use the chemical for one of our products to discourage accidental poisoning."

Luke took up the conversation then, though he didn't address Nia. Instead, his full attention was on Val. "So the chemical didn't come from some mysterious shadowy figure."

Val scowled and didn't answer.

"You understand this is going to move you up to the prime suspect slot in the murder investigation," Luke said. "Now that we know you had to ask your sister for the chemical you used in the coffee. Were you hoping to commit the murder by poisoning?"

Val dropped his arms. "I wasn't trying to kill anyone. It didn't even make anyone sick. It tasted bad, that's all."

"But what was the point?" Scarlett asked.

Val walked over and flopped into an overstuffed chair. "You don't know what it's like to work for Libby. She's a horrible boss, and she yells at me because I get sick sometimes. I work hard. I don't deserve to be treated that badly."

"If you have a bad boss," Scarlett said, "you quit. You don't poison people."

"It wasn't poison," Val whined.

"Actually, it can make some people really sick," Nia said. "At least some anecdotal evidence suggests people can be allergic to denatonium benzoate."

Val rolled his eyes. "No one started scratching so I think it was fine. I wanted Libby to get some bad reviews about her coffee, that's all. She's so proud of the stuff."

"Exactly how much of your statement to the police was a lie?" Luke asked. "Did you even get a second note? Did you switch off the lights as some kind of prank too?"

"No," Val insisted. "There was a second note. I figured Myers Portland wanted to ruin his wife's night if she wouldn't listen to him. I thought maybe she was scared of the dark or something. I didn't know, but that second envelope had a whole bunch of money in it and it didn't sound dangerous. It was the lights in one room only."

"But you don't have the note to prove it," Luke pointed out.

"Someone stole it. You saw the apartment. It took hours to get this place even halfway normal again."

"Hours of me doing most of the work," Nia grumbled.

"I hope you're telling me the truth," Luke said as he stood. "I am going to report your prank to the police. They'll decide what to do about it. You can expect to hear from them."

Val groaned, and Scarlett felt no sympathy for him at all. She did, however, feel sorry for Nia, who continued to hover fretfully.

"Nia," Scarlett asked. "Was it okay for you to bring some of that chemical home with you?"

Nia's wide-eyed gaze shifted to Scarlett. "No one at work would care—well, normally. But if this reaches the press, I'll be in a lot of trouble. It doesn't really matter that there was no rule against it. The company will be eager to find a scapegoat."

"I don't think the police make a habit of chatting with the press about this sort of thing," Scarlett said, though she also knew that gossip slipped out of even the tightest system.

Luke took a step closer to Val. "Last chance to tell me any other important information you've been keeping to yourself."

Val held up his hands. "There's nothing else. Nothing at all."

"I hope that's the truth." Luke tipped his head to Nia. "It was nice to meet you."

Nia nodded. Scarlett admired that about her. There was no way that meeting them had been a nice experience.

When they were back in the car, Luke asked, "Does eliminating the chemical clue help you feel more comfortable about Myers as prime suspect? I don't think Val murdered Tasha."

"I agree," Scarlett said. "But I'm still not sure I think Myers did either. There's something about him that makes me doubt. Maybe it's because he's too obviously the best suspect. I know that doesn't make much sense, but it's how I feel."

"No," Luke said. "I know what you mean. Myers is almost too easy. Not that killers are necessarily smart, but I can't help feeling we've been led, and I don't appreciate it."

"I don't suppose there's anything we can do?" Scarlett said, allowing hope to creep into her tone.

"One thing. The chief has given me a pass to see Tasha Portland's home. They've been over the place and didn't find anything useful, but maybe having a sense of the woman will help. You want to go with me tomorrow?" He took her hand. "Having you with me gives me an out-of-the-box perspective. That helps more than I can say."

Luke squeezed her hand, and Scarlett's breath caught in her throat, certain he was finally ready to tell her about his promotion and the move it would require. She'd been waiting for it, needing to hear it, but she was suddenly terrified that he was going to say it. So she blurted, "That sounds great. I want to see Tasha's home."

Luke's tone softened. "Good. Then how about I pick you up at the museum around midmorning? Will you be free then?"

"Free as a bird," she said with a false cheer that made her heart hurt.

20

On Tuesday morning, Scarlett left for work with a clear plan. She would focus on her job until Luke showed up. She would not fret about the murder. She would not talk about the murder. She would work. She even skipped her usual stop at Burial Grounds to head straight for her office.

She almost managed to stick to the plan. As soon as she booted up her computer, she found a flood of emails waiting for her from worried museum curators asking about the objects they'd loaned to the museum for the special exhibit. News of the murder was out.

Scarlett should have already had a carefully-worded reply ready, but she'd been so distressed over the whole situation that it hadn't even occurred to her. She decided to go with what the police believed had happened—that the incident involved a domestic issue and had nothing to do with the exhibit, and that the culprit was in custody. She assured each curator that she'd seen their particular item and it was completely untouched. To the museum that owned the sculpture that had held the bloody cloth, she settled for *undamaged* over *untouched* as the more honest answer.

She sent the last of the emails as someone knocked on her door. Certain it was Allie bringing her a much-needed cup of coffee, Scarlett sang out, "Come on in. You're a lifesaver."

The door opened, and Angelique Milston walked in with a bemused smile on her lips. "That is a much warmer reception than I expected."

Scarlett stood, feeling her cheeks warm. "Sorry about that. I thought you were Allie Preston. She often drops by around now."

"I remember her from the party," Angelique said. "She brought up coffee. I agree—she is a lifesaver."

Scarlett gestured at one of the leather-clad chairs near her desk. "Would you care to sit?"

"Thank you." Angelique took a seat and studied the room. "I was in here during the questioning, but somehow this room feels friendlier now. Perhaps it's the absence of a scowling police chief."

After a few moments, Scarlett asked, "How may I help you?"

Angelique locked eyes with Scarlett. "I heard the police arrested Myers. Does that mean the case is closed?"

"I doubt it," Scarlett said. "Though it may be soon."

"I hope so." Angelique's shoulders relaxed. "I can't say I'm sorry Tasha is dead, as that would be a lie, but I'm glad the police have found her killer."

Scarlett raised her eyebrows. "That is a rather odd thing to say. Did you have a specific problem with Tasha?"

Angelique shook her head, though it was less a denial than warding off the question. "I was worried that Rupert was developing an interest in her. I didn't think there was anything actually going on between them, exactly. But Tasha was lovely, and I suppose I worried that Rupert was losing interest in me—maybe shopping around for a younger model."

Scarlett wished she could give the woman some comfort, but she had no idea of the state of Angelique's marriage. Then she remembered something Maya had said. "Maya told me she didn't think you had anything to worry about."

"What would Maya know?" Angelique asked. "She's never been married. As far as I can tell, she doesn't know anything about men. She thinks she's this super brain."

Scarlett was surprised by the hostility in Angelique's voice. "You don't like Maya?"

Angelique waved a hand. "She's always watching and doesn't talk much. But I can tell she thinks she's smarter than me."

Scarlett suspected Angelique would be right about that, but merely said, "She has always been pleasant to me."

"Oh, she's not unpleasant," Angelique acceded. "She's simply uninteresting." Then she made a dramatic display of checking a sparkling watch on her wrist. "Well, I really should go. I mostly wanted to know if the rumors I heard about Myers were true. Do you want me to stop at Burial Grounds on my way out and tell Allie you need a coffee?"

Scarlett was surprised by the offer. "Thank you, but no. Allie doesn't need to wait on me. I'll go down after a while."

"As you wish," Angelique said, sweeping to her feet. "I'm sure I'll see you at the next museum function. I intend to continue to support this museum. I wanted you to know that."

"Thank you, and thank you for stopping by," she said. "You're always welcome."

Angelique nodded, then left.

Scarlett sank into her chair. With the emails done, her next task was to find a piece in the storage rooms that could substitute for Maya's painting. She still held hope that Maya would change her mind about taking the painting from the exhibit. Maybe, like Angelique, she'd be comforted to know the police had arrested Myers, as well as their belief that the murder had nothing to do with any scheme to steal art. Since the special exhibit room was still a crime scene, there was time for Maya to change her mind.

With a sigh, Scarlett stood again and grabbed a binder of inventory from one of the bookshelves that lined the walls. Though the inventory for the basement storage could be found in spreadsheets on her computer, she found it was easier to carry the binder. She'd taken it down a number of times as she went through the museum's stored items and jotted notes about them. Something about the physical work of making notes on paper felt like a link to her experiences on dig sites.

She was flipping through the pages, making a check mark next to potential pieces with a pencil, when another rap came at her door. She held her place in the row she'd been going over with her pencil and called, "Come in." She didn't add a cute quip this time, though she still hoped it was Allie.

The person who stepped through the door was carrying tall cups of Burial Grounds coffee, but it wasn't Allie. Luke wore his usual neat dark suit and the smile that never failed to quicken Scarlett's breath. He held out a cup. "I stopped to grab a coffee and Allie said you hadn't had one yet. She's been too busy to come up, and so she sent me."

"The museum has been unusually busy," Scarlett said as she took the coffee. "I'm told Greta and Hal are being run off their feet. I wish I thought it was the museum's collection that was drawing so much attention."

"People are curious by nature," Luke said mildly.

"That's true." Scarlett sipped the coffee. "This is wonderful. Thanks."

"Happy to oblige." Luke gestured toward the binder on her desk. "Do you still want to go with me to Tasha's house, or are you caught up in something?"

"Nothing that can't wait." Scarlett closed the binder with the pencil inside. "Let's go see what we can see."

Though on lower ground, Tasha's house was less than a mile from Maya's place. Tasha's house would obviously have views of the water, but they couldn't possibly be as spectacular as those Maya's cliffside home offered.

Luke let them into the house, and Scarlett was immediately struck by the silence inside. Somehow there was nothing more profoundly empty than an empty house. They walked together through the rooms, their footsteps loud in the space. The house was sparsely furnished in a mixed bag of Asian-inspired decor, though the selection appeared almost haphazard, which resulted in a jarring clash of color and design in some places.

"What do you think?" Luke asked in a large open-concept living area. The ceilings were vaulted, and the windows offered views of the water as Scarlett had expected.

"It's beautiful in its own way," Scarlett hedged. She stood in the middle of the room, trying to decide what bothered her so much about the place. "But it feels blank."

Luke laughed, then waved a hand toward a deep-red sofa before a heavily embroidered folding screen. Across from the sofa, a wicker chair was piled with throw pillows in jewel tones. "Blank?"

"Maybe what I meant was impersonal," Scarlett said. "Everything is styled. It's a home staged for a sale, not somewhere I can imagine a person living day to day. The table near the front door has no mail tossed on it. There's no place for someone to set their keys. Those pillows on that chair are arranged, for all that they are meant to look tossed. It's perfect, but not lived in."

"So you don't think Tasha actually lived here?" Luke asked, his face bright with interest.

"I'm not saying that, though I don't think she spent much time in this area for sure. She was into real estate, so maybe she preferred this kind of sterile room." Then she pointed at one wall. "Though that's odd to me."

"What's odd?" Luke apparently didn't see what Scarlett saw.

"There's a light shining on a blank wall," she explained. "And check out the furniture. It's arranged to face that wall. Something goes there—something special—but nothing is actually there."

Luke shrugged. "Maybe that's some new decorating trend. Imagining the art that could go there."

Scarlett laughed. "If that's a trend, I've never heard of it. I don't think decorating normally works that way. I suppose it's possible that Tasha was simply searching for the perfect piece for that spot, but I'm certain she intended it for something specific." She scanned the room again, then said, "I want to see Tasha's bedroom. Maybe she kept her personal stuff in there."

"We can check."

They began opening doors, but before they found Tasha's bedroom, they opened a door into what was obviously her home office. The room was far less sterile than the living room, though shelves lining the wall held another mixed collection of Asian art pieces. However, the desk seemed to intrigue Luke the most. He picked up a small pile of mail and leafed through several envelopes before setting them down.

"At least I can tell she actually spent time in here," Scarlett said as she paused to examine a delicate watercolor painting on the wall. She recognized the artist and whistled under her breath. "She didn't mind spending money on art."

"No?" Luke asked. "Is that valuable? It's pretty."

"Pretty and pricey." She pointed at the desk. "I don't suppose there's an appointment book?"

"There is, but the police have it. I've seen it. Nothing jumped out at me. Tasha had a busy life, but nothing suspicious."

They moved on and eventually found the bedroom. It reflected Tasha marginally better than the rest of the house. Like the office, the walls weren't as high in there, and Scarlett spotted another watercolor by the same artist as the one in the office. This one hung over the perfectly made platform bed. Tasha's clothes were neatly hung in a huge walk-in closet. Nothing was strewn around the floor or even the furniture—not clothes or even shoes.

"I'm beginning to think Tasha was pathologically neat," Scarlett said. "Either that, or I should feel a lot worse about my house."

"Your house is great," Luke said. "It's comfortable."

"Is that a nice way of saying messy?"

"No, it's a truthful way of saying comfortable. It's obvious you live there and love living there. That immediately makes your guests feel more at ease when they enter your space."

Scarlett had to admit that if she had to choose between Tasha's showplace and her own house with the kicked-off shoes in her closet and the occasional clinging cat hairs, she'd pick her place every time. "I wouldn't mind seeing the yard," Scarlett said. "Is that within the tour?"

"It can be." They went to the great room and exited through a set of sliding doors onto a flagstone patio space, complete with more Asian-inspired furniture. Scarlett paid the patio scant attention as she continued toward the water. The ground slanted down steeply at the end of the yard, but with care, a person could probably make their way to the beach below. Maybe not in the low heels Scarlett had worn to work, but she could make it okay in her hiking boots.

She glanced to the right and left, then followed the curve of land that rose toward Maya's house. Scarlett could make out the place from her current location, though Maya's home was partially hidden by trees. "I find it interesting that Maya and Tasha were such close neighbors, but not actually friends."

"They were busy people," Luke said. "I like my neighbors, but I can't say I'm close to many of them. I'm gone so much."

"That makes sense," Scarlett admitted, forcing herself not to think about how soon Luke would be gone permanently. "We know Tasha wasn't close with Angelique. I wonder if she had any female friends, or any friends at all." The thought made her sad. She was capable of burying herself in her work to the point where she shut out the world, but she'd learned so much from her time in Crescent Harbor. Now that she had good, close friends, she couldn't imagine living without them. It must be so lonely.

They both heard the sound of a car pulling up in front of the house, and Luke headed toward the noise with Scarlett following close on his heels.

They found Chief Rodriguez climbing out of his car. "I hoped I'd find you two here," he said.

"Do you need something?" Luke asked.

The chief nodded. "A murder weapon."

Luke stared at him in surprise. "You didn't think I'd find that here, did you? How would it have gotten here from the museum?"

"No, but I hoped you'd find something to point me in the right direction. We've searched the entire floor of the museum, but we haven't found anything but that bloody cloth."

"Are the test results back on that?" Luke asked.

"They are. It was Tasha's blood," the chief said. "Which we did not find on any of Libby Proctor's knives. We checked the one she said she was cut with. It had traces of blood near the handle, but like the blood on her jacket and shoe, it was hers." He ran a hand through his mop of gray hair in a gesture that was jerky with frustration. "I don't suppose you want to stick your hand into any other priceless artifacts and pull out a knife for me?"

"I wouldn't know where to begin," Scarlett said.

"Did the autopsy not reveal anything helpful?" Luke asked.

"Helpful remains to be seen, but interesting it definitely was," the chief said. "The coroner said there were traces of some kind of exotic wood in the wound. Desert ironwood to be exact, which is used by carvers. I asked if the traces could have come from the knife's handle, but he said they came from the blade itself. And what makes that especially interesting is that the blood on the cloth also included a few splinters of the same wood. I asked Myers Portland if he was into carving, but he says not."

"I don't know that anyone would carve ironwood as a casual hobby," Scarlett said. "The wood is hard to come by and expensive. It's protected by the Mexican government because the tree grows so slowly, so there's concern about overharvesting. I understand hand carving it is quite difficult, though not impossible. The carvings are a Mexican tradition."

"Myers was married to a rich woman until the divorce," the chief pointed out. "So he could have gotten the wood then."

"And he was whittling the day of the murder to pass the time?" Scarlett asked.

"I'm starting to sound desperate, aren't I?" the chief asked. "The problem is that the clues don't fit together. I'm grateful for you two solving the riddle of the chemical in the coffee, but I'm still stuck with wood in the dead woman's wound, and no murder weapon. I have plenty of people who had problems with the victim, including her ex-husband, but I'll never get a conviction with the mess we've got."

"I wish I could help," Scarlett said sincerely.

"I don't suppose you have a wooden spear in the museum's collection. Something you didn't tell me about? Preferably something stored in that utility hallway where Myers could have grabbed it for the murder?"

"I don't have an ironwood spear or dagger in the entire museum collection," Scarlett said. "And I'm not certain someone could have used the door to the hallway without anyone in the room hearing it. That door makes a scraping sound when moved."

"In the sudden pitch dark, people easily may have been too disoriented to notice," the chief said.

"I wasn't," Luke said firmly. "My first concern was Scarlett, but I've had plenty of time on the job. I'm not disoriented that easily. If there had been a scraping sound, I would have noticed, and I would have remembered."

Scarlett hadn't thought of that, and she could have smacked herself in the head at the realization. Sure, she might have been too distracted by the darkness and her worry about the guests and the artifacts, but Luke wouldn't have been. That meant no one opened and closed the rear door. And if no one came in or left, then searching the people in the room should have revealed the murder weapon. Since the murder weapon hadn't been on anyone's person, then it had to be in the exhibit room. It really was as simple as that, despite how she'd tried to make it more complicated.

And if an ironwood blade was in the exhibit room, Scarlett suddenly knew exactly where it was. "I know how the killer got the weapon into the exhibit," she said. "I know where it is now. And I think I can prove it."

As the men gaped at her, she desperately hoped she was right.

21

Scarlett stood outside the special exhibit room, sipping a cup of coffee. She didn't need it. She was shaky enough, but the hot coffee reminded her somehow that she wasn't alone. That helped her hold calm around her like a thin blanket. Underneath, she was terrified.

At least the museum is closed. What she was doing was risky, but none of their patrons could be injured. Scarlett pushed down the reminder that there was merely one person who could easily be injured in her plan—her. "Just part of the job," she whispered.

She raised the cup to her lips again and drained the last few drops of coffee. Then she practiced taking long, slow breaths until she heard the click of heels on the stairs. *Showtime.*

When Maya Shepherd appeared at the top of the stairs, her expression didn't hold her usual serenity. She was annoyed, and it showed. "What do you want? And why were you so mysterious over the phone?"

"I'm sorry," Scarlett said. "Someone walked into my office as I made the call. I didn't want to talk about your painting in front of anyone. I know you're protective of it."

Maya's forehead wrinkled, and she eyed the police caution tape in front of the exhibit door. "What about my painting?"

"I've finally impressed upon the police that several of the objects in the exhibit don't belong to this museum. You're not the only one who isn't comfortable leaving things with us right now, and I need to get everyone's art returned to them. The police have agreed to release the pieces that don't belong to the museum."

Maya visibly relaxed. "That's good news. I'll have some of my people come and pack up the painting for transport."

"No, not yet," Scarlett said. "The police still won't let outside parties into the crime scene. To be honest, I think they're getting desperate. They haven't found the murder weapon, and I think the chief of police is getting a lot of pressure to wrap it up."

"I don't understand what that has to do with my painting," Maya said.

"The chief told me that all of the pieces that need to be returned to owners right now will be removed under my supervision and taken to the police lab for one last check before they're sent to the owners. I'll oversee the whole thing to ensure the safety of every piece. Nothing will go wrong on my watch."

Maya had been shaking her head throughout Scarlett's recitation. When she spoke, her voice was louder than Scarlett had ever heard. "That is not acceptable. I told you that no one other than me or my people would be allowed to touch my painting. Period. It's in our contract."

"Yes, and I've read through the contract carefully," Scarlett said. "It is binding on the museum, but the police are not part of the museum. I know you're worried, but this is actually good news. You'll be getting your painting back, and soon."

"No," Maya said, almost shaking with fury. "I do not accept those terms."

"It's not ideal, I know."

"No, it is impossible."

Scarlett held out her hands. "I'm sorry. There is nothing I can do."

Maya was breathing hard, and Scarlett watched carefully as the furious woman began to calm herself. It was like watching someone struggling to close an overstuffed suitcase.

"I will be calling my lawyer," Maya said, her tone nearly normal.

The effect was eerie after seeing her rage mere seconds before. "I will have this stopped."

"Calling your lawyer is probably a good idea," Scarlett said. "But in this case, I'm not sure how effective it will be. The chief is sending officers over right now. That's why I called you here. I think I can talk the officers into letting you oversee the packing of your painting. It's the best I can do, but it will help you ensure that their treatment of the painting is careful and respectful."

Maya visibly trembled as she stared at the door. "If there is nothing I can do to change this situation, then I would appreciate some time alone with my painting. It's my link to my father, and I've been extremely careful with it ever since his death." Maya locked eyes with Scarlett. "Surely you owe me at least that much, since you're not planning to honor our original agreement."

"None of this was my idea," Scarlett lied smoothly. She waved a hand toward the bright yellow tape. "As you can see, the special exhibit room is still technically a crime scene."

"But you said yourself that the police are about to let you in," Maya said. "And that you believe they will let me in as well."

"Yes, probably."

"All I wish to do is to spend a moment with the painting," Maya said. "I do not visit my father's grave often, but I do tend to speak to him when I'm with the painting. I know that probably sounds silly."

"It doesn't sound silly at all. I understand perfectly. Go ahead, but you'll need to be out before the officers get here. If they see we've entered the crime scene, I'll never be able to get them to let you oversee the packing."

"Of course," Maya said with obvious relief. "I won't need long."

Scarlett lifted the crime scene tape, and Maya ducked under it. "Remember," Scarlett whispered, "be quick."

Maya nodded and let herself into the exhibit. The second the door closed behind the other woman, Scarlett sprinted for the door into the hall behind the exhibit. In the hall, Luke waited near the special exhibit door with two police officers and Winnie.

Winnie held up a computer tablet and motioned Scarlett closer. On the tablet, a live video feed was displayed from a camera that now pointed directly at Maya's painting. Maya stood in front of the painting, studying it intensely.

Scarlett clenched her fists, hoping that her theory was right. Her body tensed as she mentally urged Maya on. *Go for it. Do it.* Sure enough, Maya reached up and began fiddling with the frame of the painting near the bottom. She tugged, and a long, thin piece of wood slid out of the ornate frame.

"Now," Luke said and the police officers burst through the door and into the exhibit.

Maya froze in shock, holding the ironwood stiletto—the one she'd used to kill Tasha Portland.

Once the police took possession of the murder weapon, cuffed Maya, and read her rights, Scarlett and Winnie were allowed into the room.

Maya narrowed her eyes when she saw Scarlett. "I didn't think you were the devious type. I'm impressed." She jerked her head toward Luke. "I assume this was his idea."

"Actually it wasn't," Luke said. "It was Scarlett who figured out that the one place left to hide a murder weapon, specifically a wooden murder weapon, was in the frame of your painting."

"Clever Scarlett," Maya sneered. "Well, I'm not sorry for what I've done. I would have killed Tasha even if I'd known I wouldn't get away with it."

"But why?" Scarlett asked. "I understand Angelique's problem with Tasha, but what could she have done to make you want to kill her?"

"She was blackmailing me," Maya said.

"For what?" Scarlett asked, her mind reeling. What could Maya have done that Tasha could possibly hold over her? She expected Luke to step in and take over the questioning, but again he was letting Scarlett lead, trusting her.

"Were you aware that she dabbled in real estate?" Maya asked, the word *dabbled* positively dripping with scorn. "She was selling a property my father had designed. She discovered it was built with inferior materials, well below code. Ignoring codes can be fatal in an earthquake-prone area."

"Was this something your father had done?" Scarlett asked.

"No! My father would never have endangered people. *Never.* He was innocent. He didn't deal directly with the buying of materials, only the design. He wasn't at fault, but Tasha said she'd have no problem pointing the finger his way. She said she would make sure of it." Maya paused. She was shaking again, barely able to control herself. "She knew how much my father meant to me."

"You didn't want his name destroyed," Scarlett said.

"I couldn't allow it."

"But why would Tasha do that?" Scarlett asked.

Maya laughed mirthlessly. "She was evil."

"It had to be more than that."

"Hardly. Tasha said she couldn't see what difference it would make since my father was dead, but then she offered to protect Father's name in exchange for this painting. She thought it would go perfectly with the decor in her house. She treated the most important thing in the world to me as if it were nothing but a decoration she coveted."

"How did you get the frame made so quickly?" Luke asked.

"I didn't," Maya said. "The frame has been with the painting since my father bought it. He often said the frame was as much art as the painting. He showed me how the weapon slotted into the bottom, hiding it perfectly. He tried to learn who had originally commissioned the frame but he never could. Someone far more violent than he."

"Someone more like you," Scarlett suggested.

Maya tipped her head toward Scarlett. "Perhaps. It was perfect for my needs. All I had to do was loan it to you for the exhibit. I told Tasha that letting the museum display the painting for a brief time before I handed it over to her would make it easier on me. I viewed it as a public tribute to the painting. She agreed immediately, as that kind of attention would make the painting even more valuable."

"So the loan was simply to bring murder to my museum," Scarlett said.

Maya lifted one shoulder in a shrug. "I chose the museum because I know this place so well. I came here often when Father was working with Devon on the addition. I may know this place as well as you do. It made everything easier, though I was sorry that I had to taint my memories of this museum. Still, it was necessary. Then all I had to do was send an anonymous note to Myers, telling him about the museum party and suggesting it might be his chance to impress Tasha. I laid out a whole plan for him."

"You're very fond of anonymous messages," Scarlett said. "You called me on the night of the murder, didn't you?"

"I did," Maya said. "As I said, I felt guilty."

"But not guilty enough not to end someone's life," Luke said.

"No," Maya snapped. "I'll never be sorry for that. If ever anyone deserved to die, it was Tasha Portland."

"I still don't quite understand how you did it," Scarlett said. "How could you know where Tasha was? Or didn't you care if you hurt or killed the wrong person?"

Maya snorted. "Don't be dramatic. I made a point of watching her as we went into the exhibit. I knew once the lights were off, she'd be unlikely to move in the perfect darkness. I have an excellent memory."

"Still, that was risky," Scarlett said.

Maya beamed at that as if Scarlett had given her a compliment. "It was necessary. And the cell phone lights didn't make it easier, but I was quick, grabbing the knife from the frame and doing the job within seconds of the lights going out."

"Then you wiped the blade on a cloth," Luke said.

"One I'd brought with me for the task. I couldn't risk putting a bloody knife into the frame. The police would find it. I left the cloth in here. I knew once Tasha's body was discovered, we would all be searched."

"Yes, we found it. In fact, it helped to crack the case," Scarlett said. "But how did you get your note away from Val? Was the whole break-in at his apartment staged?"

"No, it was hired," Maya said. "I detest hiring the sort of person who searches apartments, but I couldn't be in two places at once, and I couldn't risk anyone seeing that note in case my detailed directions gave me away somehow." She chuckled, a cold sound. "Fortunately, I wasn't the only one sending the kid notes with money."

"If you were concerned about leaving notes behind, why leave one in my car?"

Maya shrugged. "It was a risk, but the note was shorter, and you were kind enough to leave the doors unlocked. I didn't think it would give me away. Besides, I simply had to gloat to someone. I couldn't stand the thought of anyone lauding that woman. She deserved to die."

"No," Scarlett said firmly. "No one deserves to be murdered."

Maya laughed, and the noise sent a shiver down Scarlett's spine. "I suppose we will simply have to agree to disagree."

"I think we've heard enough for now," Luke said. "It's time for you to go."

"I understand." Maya faced Scarlett one last time. "If I'd given Tasha my painting, it wouldn't have been enough. She'd never have stopped taking from me. In the end, my father protected me. Don't you think there is something poetic there?"

"No," Scarlett said. "Not poetic. But sad, terribly sad."

And with that, the police urged Maya along out of the exhibit while all the ancient depictions of women looked on.

22

Scarlett didn't see Luke again on Tuesday, though he texted several times, keeping her abreast of the process and assuring her that he missed her. She missed him too, but the break gave Scarlett time to process her feelings about the murder. Fortunately, she had plenty of people ready to process it with her.

Allie practically bowled Scarlett over on Wednesday morning. "Why didn't you call me?" she demanded. "You solved a murder without me and didn't even call?"

"Sorry," Scarlett said. "I was exhausted."

"I'm in a forgiving mood." Allie linked her arm in Scarlett's and towed her toward Burial Grounds. "All you have to do is come in here and tell us everything."

"Us?" Scarlett asked.

Greta poked her head out the doorway of the coffee shop and waved. Her bright face made Scarlett laugh. Her friends certainly loved a mystery.

"I'm surprised you didn't ask Winnie," Scarlett said as Allie dragged her into the coffee shop.

"We did," Greta told her. "But she wouldn't say anything."

"I knew you were easier to pressure," Allie said.

"I'm not sure I appreciate that," Scarlett said, but she quickly gave in and told Allie and Greta about Maya's arrest. She didn't feel sorry for Maya. The woman's coldness had been chilling, but she could understand Maya's loyalty to her father. How would Scarlett herself react if someone tried to sully her father's name?

"Well, I wouldn't murder them," Greta said when Scarlett voiced her thoughts aloud.

"I don't know," Allie said. "I might. No one messes with my family."

Scarlett held up her hands in mock horror. "I'll keep that in mind."

"Speaking of family," Greta said. "Don't forget Hal and I are hosting our usual Christmas party at the end of this week. I assume we'll see you there."

"Of course," Scarlett said, trying not to let on that she'd forgotten the party was so close. But they were barely a week away from Christmas Day. The thought made her sad as she immediately pictured Luke having his last Christmas with his family before he'd be moving away from them and her.

"Scarlett?" Allie said. "You okay?"

Scarlett forced a smile. "I guess I'm tired. It's been a lot lately."

"Don't worry," Greta said, giving Scarlett a pat on the arm. "We'll cheer you up at the Christmas party. No one can stay sad at one of our parties."

"I'll be fine by then," Scarlett promised Greta, hoping it was the truth. She slipped away with a cup of coffee to throw herself into some work. All day she wondered if Luke would pop by her office, but he didn't, though he did call as the museum closed.

"Do you mind if I swing by your place tonight?" he asked.

"Is this a new thing?" she asked. "You actually asking before you surprise me?"

"I thought I'd try it on for a change. Besides, I think you've had enough surprises lately."

"That's how life is," Scarlett said. "Full of surprises. Of course you can come over. I can't think of anything I'd enjoy more." *Though if you're coming to tell me that you're leaving, I'm probably lying.*

"I'll be there." A muffled voice called his name in the background, and Luke replied that he'd be right there. "Gotta run. See you tonight."

"I'll see you," she said.

After the museum closed for the day, Scarlett stopped to treat herself to a quick baked chicken dinner before heading home, making sure to bring a piece home with her as a special treat for Cleo. When she got home, Cleo raced up to greet her and Scarlett scooped up the cat. She stood near the door and surveyed her open living space. "You can't even tell it's almost Christmas here," she said.

Cleo meowed, either in agreement or in demand for the food she could probably smell in Scarlett's bag. It was hard to tell with Cleo. Scarlett went with the safe guess and carried Cleo to the kitchen. While Cleo investigated her bit of chicken, Scarlett slapped a hand on the counter, making the cat jump.

"I've made up my mind," she told the reproachful cat. "I need some Christmas spirit in here."

Cleo merely buried her face in her food while Scarlett strode off to the spare bedroom closet where she stored the Christmas decorations she'd brought with her when she moved from New York. She had considered tossing them since she'd so rarely used them in New York, but she'd never been able to bring herself to do it. Cleo often saw Christmas trees as a challenge, but Scarlett didn't care. She wanted—no, needed—something festive, something to remind her that Christmas was a happy time.

She hauled her small artificial tree into the living room and set it up between the fireplace and a bank of windows. Cleo came into the room as Scarlett slotted in the last of the branches. The cat sat on the ottoman to watch. Scarlett pointed at her. "You leave this tree alone."

Cleo yawned, unimpressed by the warning, and began washing her face as if she had no interest in the tree at all. Scarlett began hanging her collection of unbreakable ornaments on the tree. As she worked, Cleo finished her wash and curled up for a nap. Scarlett hummed Christmas songs, surprised to find that the simple act of hanging ornaments was cheering her up.

The doorbell drew her away, and she wove through the ornament boxes to open the door.

Luke stood in the entryway and held up a bottle of champagne. "I thought we could celebrate the closing of the case."

"Sounds good," Scarlett said. "Come in. I assume everything is settled with Maya."

Luke carried the bottle to the kitchen as Scarlett collected a pair of champagne flutes from the cabinet. "She's been very forthcoming. I think she's actually proud of it." He popped the cork and filled the glasses.

"How awful. I assume Maya threw the rock at the camera." Scarlett took a glass from him.

"No. Apparently that was in the note of instructions she gave Val. It was a happy coincidence since she had no idea Myers would be let in that door. She simply directed Val to knock one of the cameras out of position to muddy the waters during the investigation and suggest that someone might have come in."

"Interesting that Val didn't tell us that," Scarlett said before sipping her champagne.

"He's been asked about it and says he forgot. He seems to have a poor memory when it comes to criminal acts. That young man is going to have a lot to answer for."

"So the murder investigation is wrapped up," Scarlett said. "And all very sad."

"Murder tends to be, but it's good to have the truth." He held up the champagne flute. "To truth."

Scarlett raised her own glass and echoed the sentiment, but the words gave her a pang of guilt. "I have something to confess."

Luke set his glass down on the counter. "Confess?"

"You remember when you let me bring your car home after we discovered the mess at Val's house?"

"I do."

"Well, I saw a letter in your car, and I remembered what the chief had said about a promotion, which you weren't exactly forthcoming about. So I read it. I'm sorry. I know it was wrong, but why didn't you tell me you're moving?"

Luke blinked in surprise. "Moving?"

"To Virginia." She huffed in exasperation. "I read the letter. I know the promotion comes with a position in Virginia."

"And you assumed I was taking it?" He smiled at her when she nodded and gently took the glass from her hand, setting it beside his own. "I am constantly surprised by you. You see things I can never catch, but you miss some of the most obvious stuff right under your nose. Tell me, Scarlett, if you were offered a promotion that took you to Virginia, would you take it?"

Scarlett considered that for a moment. Then shook her head. "I don't want to leave Crescent Harbor. It's been an adventure and not always an enjoyable one, but it's one that's changed me. I feel at home here."

"As do I," Luke said. "Crescent Harbor is my home, now more than ever. I turned down the promotion because I would never, ever take a job that took me away from you. You're the most important person in my life. You're the most important person who has ever been in my life. I love you, Scarlett McCormick."

Scarlett felt as if her heart might burst from her chest. "I love you too."

"I'm sorry you've been feeling as if I'm about to abandon you. I have been keeping something from you, but it's the opposite of abandonment. I've been distant because I've been worried that this wouldn't be ready in time, but now that it is, I don't want to wait until Christmas to give it to you."

To Scarlett's shock, he knelt in front of her, pulling a small box from his pocket. A solitaire diamond sparkled up at her, nestled in a white-gold setting that featured ornate filigree. "When I asked your father's blessing months ago, he also told me where you had your first in-field archaeological dig. I contacted the people in charge of the site now, and they sold me one of the diamonds from that site. I had it shipped to a jeweler here, who was able to fit it into an antique ring that's been passed down in my family for generations. To me, this ring is symbolic of both of our histories being combined into one life—our life together. Scarlett, will you marry me?"

Tears had filled her eyes and begun to trickle down her cheeks as he spoke. Her heart felt as if it would burst as she whispered, "Yes, I will."

Beaming, he slid the ring onto her finger, then took her face in his hands and kissed her, long and slow.

Scarlett was almost giddy with joy when she heard a loud, complaining yowl. Luke released her, and she peered down at the floor where Cleo was staring up at them in clear annoyance.

"Sorry, Cleo," Luke said. "You're going to have to get used to sharing." He kissed Scarlett again, and if Cleo complained any more, neither of them could hear it.